1Wanumm

Birds Every Child Should Know

Neltje Blanchan

BiRDS
EVERY
CHiLD
SHOULD
KNOW

*Illustrations
by Christine Stetler*

University of Iowa Press　Ψ　Iowa City

University of Iowa Press, Iowa City 52242
Copyright © 2000 by the University of Iowa Press
All rights reserved
Printed in the United States of America
Originally published in 1907 by Doubleday, Page & Company

http://www.uiowa.edu/~uipress

Printed on acid-free paper

Library of Congress Cataloging-in-Publication Data
Blanchan, Neltje, 1865–1918.
Birds every child should know / by Neltje Blanchan.
p.   cm.
Originally published: 1907.
Summary: Describes more than 100 common United States
birds, including their physical attributes, calls, and nesting
and mating habits.
ISBN 0-87745-716-6 (cloth), ISBN 0-87745-705-0 (pbk.)
1. Birds—Juvenile literature. [1. Birds.]   I. Title.
QL676.2.B62 2000   99-057787
598—dc21

00 01 02 03 04 C 5 4 3 2 1
00 01 02 03 04 P 5 4 3 2 1

CONTENTS

FOREWORD

Cornelia F. Mutel

In 1897, a decade before this bird book for children was first published, the few remaining passenger pigeons—a species that had once constituted a quarter of all American land birds—were withering away in the Cincinnati Zoo. Already in the 1880s the nation's bird populations had dropped by an estimated 46 percent during the previous hundred years. And still Americans hailed seabirds, songbirds, any and all birds as cheap and abundant. Their flesh, steaming and succulent, adorned the dining table. Their feathers, wings, and stuffed bodies graced women's hair and hats. Birds, like any remaining usable wild animals, existed only for human use. True, their numbers were declining at alarming rates, but that was blamed in part on predators, which were seen as cruel, judged moralistically as evil, and targeted for extermination. Even nature lovers encouraged the killing of wolves and cougars, owls, hawks, and eagles.

Amidst the carnage and chaos, voices were starting to speak up. The writings of Henry David Thoreau, written nearly half a century earlier, were being rediscovered and read attentively. The many books of John Burroughs, to this day probably the most widely read naturalist in American history, were being consumed vociferously. And those of Neltje Blanchan, pen name for Nellie Blanchan DeGraff Doubleday, were starting to appear on people's shelves.

Neltje Blanchan—who was she? Few, if any, recognize her name today. Remaining copies of her books, their pages yellowing and bindings crumbling, gather dust on library shelves. Yet for a period early in the twentieth century, Blanchan's several books on birds and gardening enjoyed a wide readership. Unfortunately for us, they contained nothing about the author, no biographical sketches, no photographs. All we know of Blanchan now is what we can dig from biographical indexes of her day.

Born in 1865 in Chicago, she was educated in eastern private schools. At age twenty-one, in 1886, she became the wife of Frank Nelson Doubleday, who was to establish the family-run Doubleday publishing company eleven years hence. The marriage immediately plunged Blanchan into the world of writers and publishers, for her husband was then editor of the *Book Buyer* and later became manager of *Scribner's Magazine*. Meanwhile Blanchan produced two sons, Felix in 1887 and Nelson in 1889, and a daughter, Dorothy, in 1892. In 1894, when Dorothy was two

and Neltje twenty-nine, her first book—a dis-
course on the Piegan Indians—was published.
Thereafter her books appeared in quick succession: *Bird Neighbors* (1897), *Birds That Hunt and
Are Hunted* (1898), *Nature's Garden* (1900), *How
to Attract the Birds* (1902), *Birds Every Child
Should Know* (1907), *The American Flower Garden* (1909), and a compilation from her earlier
books, *Birds Worth Knowing* (1917).

In 1897, Frank Doubleday joined S. S. McClure
(the publisher of *McClure's Magazine*) in creat-
ing a new publishing firm, Doubleday and
McClure. Three years later that firm (which in
the year of its establishment published Blanchan's *Bird Neighbors*) transformed itself into
Doubleday, Page and Company, a forerunner of
today's Doubleday (now a division of Random
House, Inc.). Doubleday and Page rapidly slipped
into line as one of the nation's largest and most
innovative presses, and Neltje and Frank's stat-
ure blossomed accordingly, socially as well as
financially. Indeed, family friend Rudyard Kipling
nicknamed Frank "Effendi" (a play on his initials
"F. N. D.") and wrote the book *Just So Stories* in
response to story requests from the couple's son
Nelson.

The press published Kipling's books as well as
those of many other contemporaneous greats:
Booth Tarkington, Joseph Conrad, O. Henry, and
Selma Langerlöf, to name a few. It also published

all of Blanchan's subsequent books. Indeed, Blanchan credits much of her success to her husband's occupation. Her dedication in *The American Flower Garden* is inscribed, "To my husband, but for whom none of my books would ever have been published." Whether this was actually the case, we do not know. Her writings became popular for a period in the early 1900s. Most of her books went through multiple reprintings. Blanchan herself didn't hesitate to call attention in her preface to *Birds Worth Knowing* to the "several hundred thousand readers [who] have been kind enough to approve the author's four previous volumes on birds." The books, lavishly embellished with color sketches and photographs, were praised as being accurate, authoritative, and well-ordered. Written as popular guides for the amateur, they contained elementary information that was easily accessible. Blanchan's chatty, vivacious, and informed style made them readable and enjoyable as well. Thus, she ranked as one of the notable women writers on birds around the turn of the century.

In addition to her writing contributions, we can assume that she played a significant role in shaping the rapidly growing Doubleday firm and, through it, the literary atmosphere of her times. This supposition is best supported by a purported action that later won her criticism rather than praise. While the Doubledays were traveling in

Europe in 1900, the new Doubleday, Page and Company received a manuscript from a young and unpublished author, Theodore Dreiser. A reader approved the manuscript and offered a contract to Dreiser, which he accepted. When the Doubledays returned and Blanchan read the proofs, she reported her shock at the book's frank content. Her sympathetic husband was unable to withdraw the contract and was legally required to publish the book, but he chose neither to promote nor to distribute the small number of copies that he printed. Thus the later-famous *Sister Carrie* failed initially, an event that Dreiser blamed bitterly on Blanchan.

While this action may have temporarily stifled Dreiser, nothing seems to have stifled Blanchan. In addition to her several books, she wrote an abundance of magazine articles, many of which were published in Doubleday, Page and Company's *Country Life*. These articles addressed a diversity of topics: Native American education and handicrafts, literary criticism, agriculture, and antique furniture, plus numerous book reviews. And although we have no record of this, we can presume that she influenced the establishment of the press's Nature Series, which John Burroughs in Blanchan's *Bird Neighbors* praised as a competent, reliable, and readable set of volumes that were popular without being sensational. He concluded, "This library is free from the scientific dry rot on the one hand and from the florid and misleading romanticism of much recent nature writing on the other. It is a safe guide to the world of animal and plant life that lies about us. And that is all the wise reader wants."

Neltje Blanchan. We know only the slightest outline of her life events. From these, we can try to imagine the pattern of her days spent at her affluent estate, Effendi Hill, in Oyster Bay, Long Island. We can picture her here caring for little Felix, Nelson, and Dorothy, passing them on to a nursemaid when she turned to her writing. Gazing from a lavish home through windows overlooking the gardener-tended grounds, taking delight in the flitting waves of color and sound expressed in the small bodies of birds and flowers, growing to love these vibrant tidbits of life. Learning all that she could about them. Writing about them. Writing with passion and charm, giving structure to what she had learned and then pouring out that knowledge in a voice that expressed the energy within her. Churning out a book every few years, despite the callings of her family and the social obligations engendered by her husband and his thriving press. And on top of these activities, devoting much time and energy to the charitable as well as social causes appropriate for a woman of her social prominence and fitting to a woman with her concerns.

These things we can imagine. We can try to weave for ourselves a Neltje Blanchan tapestry in the corners of our mind. But perhaps she would be understood more accurately if we were to expand our understanding of the times in which she lived and place her adopted calling within the context of an era. Seen thus, her writing becomes a representative and significant expression of the influential conservation movement that marked the early twentieth century.

Settlers on this vast continent, frequently fleeing lives of deprivation, realized that they were immersed within a sea of natural abundance. Vast forests provided wood for construction and fuel and held the animals that would feed their growing families and clothe and decorate their bodies. The natural elements that would sustain life were free for the taking in unbelievable profusion. Animals and plants were here to be used and to be used up.

It's difficult to condemn the settlers for reveling in this fertility with what appears now as inexhaustible and distasteful gluttony. They were pulled by the growl of their hungry stomachs as well as by the fashions of the times, which in turn were fed by market forces and by commercial or market hunters. What we might now imagine as a natural garden was, to our predecessors, a barrier to be transformed into a tamed land perceived as less unknown, less uncontrollable, less fearful—in other words more comfortable, safe, and habitable. Their mission—to replace the wilderness with croplands and towns, to slice through the unending forest with roads—was the only goal that made sense to them. The natural world poured out such a ridiculous bounty of riches, they could not imagine that this copious fertility would ever end.

And so it happened, time and time again. Expansion tied to insatiable hunger for the land's wealth produced an orgy that destroyed the continent's abundance and then, with little thought of what was left behind, the pioneers moved on. The loggers who had reshaped the forests of New England into barns, houses, fences, and furniture migrated to Michigan, then Wisconsin and Minnesota, sending rafts of white pine a quarter mile long down the Mississippi to frame the farmsteads that would pierce the treeless prairies of the Great Plains. By 1900, when Blanchan was launching her career, the loggers had moved on to the Pacific Northwest.

Simultaneously the North American beaver population, estimated at 60 million strong at the time of European colonization, was systematically being converted into hats and coats until, in 1900, only around 100,000 remained. By that date, the lust for deerskins and venison had dropped the deer population to a few percent of its original estimate of 24 to 36 million.

Bison, which originally roamed nearly the entire U.S., probably once numbered about the same—30 million animals or so, although some say there were over twice that many. While most had vanished from east of the Mississippi River by 1820, the herds covering the western plains continued to be measured by the mile. As one Native American put it, "The country was one robe." With such numbers, it seemed that the bison could never disappear. And so it was, until the great herds were pierced by the transcontinental railroads. These allowed hunters, armed with the new mass-produced rapid-firing rifles, to kill not only for meat, moccasins, boots, and buffalo robes, but also for shear sport. Within a few decades, the great herds were gone. By 1895, fewer than a thousand bison huddled in zoos, private holdings, and parks; the single remaining wild band had fled to Canada.

Birds were not immune to the carnage. They were the victims of egg collectors and hunters. Although authors such as Blanchan lectured their readers about the numerous economic benefits of birds—their control of insects, of weed seeds, and rodents—birds were attacked as agricultural pests. The colorful Carolina parakeet, the continental U.S.'s only native parrot, which once numbered in the millions, was hunted to extinction primarily for this reason, the last pair dying in 1917. Overhunting to provide the nation's dinner tables with meat also devastated the nation's bird populations. Songbirds were served on skewers; prairie chickens were chopped into salads; teal and snipes were broiled as entrees; cedar waxwings and goldfinches were baked into pies; robin broth was served as the food of choice for invalids. Restaurant diners in Boston found plovers and curlews on the menu.

The passenger pigeon became the bird correlate of the bison. With its blue-gray head and tail, pink neck and throat, and two-foot wingspan, this pigeon symbolized abundance beyond belief. The species numbered an estimated 6 billion at the time of Euro-American settlement. Its breeding grounds might cover as many as 45 square miles. The size of flocks, measured in the tens of miles, made them easy to down. They were hunted with nets and sticks as well as with guns. Flocks were dense enough to darken the noonday sun. Alighting in trees, the birds' combined weight was great enough to split trunks two feet in diameter. These tremendous flocks were killed, crated, and cast onto freight cars destined for big city markets. By the 1880s, the birds were scarce in most areas. With the death of the last passenger pigeon in 1914, the species became extinct.

Many birds were killed for reasons far less

practical than supplying dining tables with meat. Bird feathers had trimmed clothing of aristocrats for centuries, but their limited use had been confined to a few species. This changed after 1850, when a growing, fashion-conscious middle class in both the United States and Western Europe adopted the habit of decorating clothes, especially hats, with feathers and bird parts. What we would now consider as bizarre soon came to be seen as beautiful. Feathers, entire stuffed birds, and bird parts (breasts, tails, outstretched wings) of every species imaginable—from eagles, ibis, and parakeets to tanagers and orioles—were sewn onto hats, fans, gowns, capes, parasols, and muffs. Hats might be adorned with owls' heads with blank staring eyes, small birds in attitudes of incubation, entire terns with wings outspread, or hummingbirds perched on artificial flowers, or they might bear grotesque arrangements of wings, tails, heads, and other parts of multiple species. Dresses might be hemmed with the heads of finches or edged with swallows' wings or grebes' skins.

The demand resulted in a healthy trade of feathers from native birds around the world. Bulky bales of plumes were shipped to New York, Paris, and London to quell the consumers' demands, but constantly changing millinery styles required that more and still more feathers be sought—resulting in the killing of an estimated five million birds each year for the last forty years of the nineteenth century. At least fifty North American species were hunted for the feather trade, but the white feathers of great and snowy egrets were in particularly high demand. Horrendous tales were told of their procurement. The most desired feathers were obtained during the breeding season. Hunters would thus slip up to nesting sites, shoot a volley of shot into colonies, and strip feathers from the targets within easy reach, leaving many more wounded adults along with the young to starve or be eaten. Feather dealers, some employing dozens of hunters, rapidly eliminated entire colonies of birds. Populations of shore, sea, and marsh birds in particular declined dramatically, and many feared the extinction of the egrets. Still the hunting continued, for the rewards were great: some feathers were literally worth more than their weight in gold.

And so the nation's varied wild creatures were harvested for food and fiber, fur and feather. In addition, loss of habitat took its toll on wildlife populations, as did sport hunting performed without laws or limits, spurred following the Civil War by rising incomes, more leisure time, an expanding middle class, and cheap, mass-produced rifles. And as human use transformed the land, resources once perceived as inexhaustible started their slip toward oblivion.

There had always been a few voices speaking out against this ubiquitous overconsumption of nature's bounty. However, few listened to these voices until the slaughter reached its peak. At that point, the public realized that the impossible had happened. Things that could not run out were on the run. The wilderness had vanished. The disappearance of the once incredibly abundant bison and passenger pigeon in particular shocked Americans as little else could. For the first time, Americans in the late nineteenth century reacted as a group to the loss of the wild and native.

They found their voice in part by speaking through an explosion of new organizations devoted to the preservation of wildlife and habitat. Such groups soared in number, from 34 in 1878 to 308 within a decade. If clubs interested in both hunting and conservation were counted, the number approached a thousand. From these groups flowed magazines and bulletins urging protective legislation, wildlife preserves, restraint or abstinence in the killing of non-game species, and the abolition of market hunting. Two prominent organizations focused specifically on birds. The American Ornithological Union, established in 1866, began to provide lectures, publications, scientific testimony, and legislative pressure promoting bird preservation. Perhaps more influential and representative was the

Audubon Society, with origins in individual states commencing in 1896 following an aborted initiation a decade earlier. The society had three objectives in mind: halting the killing of any wild birds not used as food, ceasing the destruction of all wild nests or eggs, and eliminating the wearing of ornamental feathers. It sought to do so by implementing an abundance and diversity of educational efforts, preservation initiatives, and legislative pressures. The society's efforts came to be recognized and praised by many. As Blanchan herself wrote in her prefaces to *Bird Neighbors* and *Birds Worth Knowing*, the Audubon Society's educational efforts were largely responsible for the "immense wave of interest in birds [that] recently swept over the country where less than a generation ago was complete indifference to their extermination." Praising the society's pamphlets and pictures, classes for children and lectures for adults, sanctuaries for breeding birds with on-site wardens to guard them, and related activities, she concluded that the Audubon Society, "more than all other agencies combined, is due the credit of eliminating so much of the Prussianlike cruelty toward birds that once characterized American treatment of them."

The cries against the loss of wildlife were intertwined with those of a major back-to-nature movement that, by 1900, was sweeping the country, forcing significant shifts in attitude and style. This movement, propelled largely by nostalgia for what had been destroyed, was both fueled by and fuel for the conservation efforts and their publications. The movement was also in part a reaction to the rapid industrialization of the country, which was cutting the masses off from their agrarian and rural roots. As conditions in urban centers worsened, city dwellers embraced the Romantic ideal of the bygone rural culture and virtues. Simultaneously, a growing standard of living supplied the more affluent segments of the population leisure time during which to re-connect to nature through botanizing, birdlore, camping, and the like. The resulting wave of na-ture sentiment and focus on nature study was de-voted to the pastoral countryside. Americans in increasing numbers journeyed to the country for the spiritual and physical health brought about by clean air and blue skies. Many thousands of children were transported to summer camps and enrolled in nature groups that taught them the skills of living in nature. Adults and families trav-eled in droves to the country to picnic and camp.

The awakening interest in nature and the rural lifestyle was exemplified through the develop-ment of Doubleday, Page and Company, which published its books under the imprint Country Life Press. In 1910, when the firm's growth out-stripped its New York City headquarters, the company turned to its founding principles. As pronounced in a 1910 in-house history of Country Life Press, "Although we had been advocating the country as a place for living and doing one's work, we still spent our efforts in . . . New York City." But when a plot of forty acres with ready train connections was found in the then-pastoral Garden City, Long Island, the entire operation was moved into a rural headquarters. Employees at this novel commercial press and warehouse were then presented with a new way of life as well as a salary. The surroundings of the large commercial building were reshaped into a parkland with 500 transplanted large cedars, 100,000 young trees and plants, iris and peony gardens, a greenhouse, a picking garden, and an orchard and vegetable garden, the fruits of which were sold to the workers at cost. When time permitted, employees could utilize the plant's large playground and tennis courts or stroll along tree-shaded lanes and admire the 100,000-gallon Italian pond.

Publications describing the company's first decades stress these natural amenities as much as the plant's modern equipment, clean workshop, and workrooms with good light, air, and sunshine, all of which led to "better spirit and work done in fewer hours and with greater cheerfulness." But the plant's immersion in nature was not just good business. It was also an expression of a moral stance and mission that had been incorporated in the corporation's "Country Life Creed," which stated efforts "to encourage country living, to draw people from the crowded cities into the open spaces, to foster a love of the wide outdoors, . . . to keep active the love of all things that live and grow," and "to inspire communion with nature in all moods" as "the sum and substance of our effort."

When Doubleday's employees—or anyone else for that matter—found that traveling to nature was impossible or inconvenient, they could turn to an outpouring of nature-oriented instructional pamphlets, books, or inexpensive nature magazines, publications that were abundant in part because of the recent availability of cheap paper and high-speed printing. These were the product of a nature-writing movement unlike anything in the past. A diversity of nature guides, stories, and travelogues for children as well as adults were published and bought in astounding quantities. Nature books too, authored by a number of popular writers, were being published in such numbers that their soaring growth was compared to the surging development of the automobile industry.

The most venerated nature author by far was John Burroughs, who by 1900 had become an icon across the country. His grandfatherly beard and angelic white hair spoke to readers of a tolerant, sunny, and endearing nature which was portrayed in his well-crafted, optimistic, and affectionate essays on the gentler creatures of the natural world. His numerous and enormously popular books established the standards for a new form of nature writing. Hundreds of thousands of copies of his books were purchased for classroom use alone.

Burroughs assisted Blanchan with her ordering of topics in her first bird book, *Bird Neighbors*. He then read and annotated the manuscript, and wrote an introduction for the book, citing it as "reliable and written in a vivacious strain and by a real bird lover." Given his immense popularity, his endorsement of her writing must have been a major boost to the acceptance of her efforts. His commendation was especially meaningful because of Burroughs's outspoken disdain for what he considered to be slipshod and sentimental nature books, a disdain that led a few years later to a major national controversy about what he considered "sham nature history" written by "nature fakers." Only a small number of realistic, knowledge-based nature books made valuable contributions to natural history literature, the formidable Burroughs argued, and he presumably placed Blanchan's writings among the chosen few.

Let's look more closely at the Blanchan reflected

in her writing. Perhaps most obviously, she was a woman actively interested in studying nature. Was this unusual? Far from it. Women of the period were viewed as the defenders of the home and child, along with the middle-class lifestyle that enfolded their families. This lifestyle embraced the exploding interest in nature appreciation and nature education. Gardens and birds were deemed crucial to the upbringing of children as well as socially appropriate topics for exploration and expression by women, in particular women of means. Many women of the late nineteenth century devoted their lives to the study and protection of nature, and a large number of these women naturalists investigated birds. Writing about birds and other nature topics was but one of several acceptable creative feminine outlets.

However, women did far more than write. Middle- and upper-class women across the nation spearheaded actions to preserve forests, water, and other amenities of nature, thus becoming paramount to the success of the conservation efforts of the times. Women activists were pivotal in the fight against killing birds for fashion. The first successful Audubon Club was formed in Massachusetts by a group of women appalled at the slaughter of birds for millinery. Many other local clubs across the country formed around the central figure of a prominent woman. Women signed pledges by the thousands vowing not to wear bird-bedecked hats and formed a Plumage League intent on ending the millinery industry's use of birds. The 1913 passage of a tariff act banning importation of wild bird feathers, an attack on the transatlantic plume trade, resulted from women's pressures.

Nature books and articles about birds spread the conservationists' message, and their educational impact about the virtues of birds was crucial to the conservation movement's success. The very influential female authors Olive Thorne Miller, Mabel Osgood Wright, and Florence A. Merriam (Bailey) had preceded Blanchan in time and surpassed her in impact and importance. These female writers joined their words to the myriad female-initiated actions that were simultaneously attacking the negative actions of overhunting, egg collection, and the use of feathers to decorate millinery and clothing, and promoting the appreciation of birds and bird watching. Thus Blanchan's interests and writing efforts were typical representations of the gender-role expectations as well as the conservation activism of the times. And the efforts of women like Blanchan had stupendous results. Environmental historian Carolyn Merchant writes, "Nowhere has women's self-conscious role as protectors of the environment been better exemplified than during the progressive conservation movement of early twentieth century," when they transformed the crusade for nature from "an elite male enterprise into a widely based movement."

And what of her writing for children? Was this unusual? Again, the answer must be a vehement no. Conservationists struggled to inculcate respect and love for the natural world and to pull children into all aspects of wildlife preservation, realizing that generating positive attitudes in the upcoming generation was equal in importance to fighting nature-destroying activities. The Audubon Society from the start provided schools with posters and instructional materials, sponsored nature clubs for children, and published children's stories, essays, and pictures in addition to plans for birdhouses. Children, whose involvement was seen as essential to the society's success, were solicited to become society members, and in 1910 the Junior Audubon Club was formed specifically for these younger partners. It barraged children with leaflets on various birds and how they should be protected, until (as Blanchan wrote in her preface to *Birds Worth Knowing*) "the making of birdhouses, fountains, and restaurants has suddenly become . . . a pastime for every boy and girl who can handle a hammer." By 1900, the study of nature had also become an important part of the elementary and secondary school curriculum and remained thus into the 1920s. Nature-oriented essays and stories

abounded, from reading primers to college reading lists and everything in between. Publications
encouraged children's active involvement in both
understanding and preserving birds and other
wildlife. Thus neither of Blanchan's two
children's volumes, this book and her earlier
How to Attract the Birds, were at all unusual.

This cultural emphasis on nature study also
explains the *should* in the title *Birds Every Child
Should Know*. When it was first published in
1907, and for many years following, children
were taught that their understanding of the natural world was important and, yes, that developing
this understanding was expected of them. The
justifications for this expectation were numerous, as Blanchan herself explains in the preface
to this volume: "Nature, the best teacher of all,
trains the child's eyes through study of the birds
to quickness and precision, which are the first
requisites for all intelligent observation in every
field of knowledge." She points out that a child's
attentiveness to birds also trains the ear, mus-
cles, imagination, and the sympathies or "the
growth of the heart," which she concludes is the
most significant attribute of all.

Neltje Blanchan. One of a number of women who
helped shape, and was shaped by, a conservation
movement whose results still benefit us today.
She would be pleased to know we are stopping to

look at her work anew, to value it, and to resurrect it. She would be pleased to know that a hundred years after she had penned her insights, nature lovers were pausing for a moment to thank her for her efforts. She might be especially pleased because she was robbed of the revel in achievement that old age may have brought her. A leading member of Long Island's Red Cross Society, in 1917 (the year that the U.S. entered World War I) she was selected by the American Red Cross for a special mission in China. She left with her husband in December. A few months later, in February 1918, the same year that her son Nelson joined the Doubleday business as junior partner, the fifty-two-year-old Blanchan died suddenly of undetermined causes in Canton. Her husband wired the news back to the States and returned to attend her memorial service at the Matinecock Neighborhood House, one of her philanthropic causes.

Well before the time of her death, Blanchan's books and myriad related publications and efforts pushed toward the establishment of agencies, programs, and legislation that safeguarded birds, as well as other wildlife. What exactly were these programs? And where do we, and the birds, stand today?

When the past century's nature lovers and hunters united in their pressure for saving wildlife, the federal government began to act.

Yellowstone, the nation's and world's first national park, was established in 1872. This served
as precedent to the establishment of parks and
preserves across the country, founded by private
organizations (such as the Audubon Society) as
well as state and federal governments. With time,
these came to serve as research and educational
sites in addition to providing habitat for native
species. Today we are reintroducing native species that were eliminated by our forebears from
such sites and also attempting to restore the native habitat that covered them a few centuries
ago.

Legislative controls helped terminate the trade
of bird plumes, and through this the plunder of
bird populations. In 1900 the U.S. Congress
passed the Lacey Act, a major success for wildlife
activists that largely choked off market hunting
for interstate shipment of wildlife or wildlife
products within a decade. The federal Migratory
Bird Treaty Act of 1918, signed by Canada and the
U.S., committed both countries to agreeing on
seasons, bag limits, and protected species of migrating waterfowl, and by 1920 state regulations
governing hunting were almost universal. The
legislative foundation of a wildlife policy had
been established.

The concept of preserving *all* species, or of an
ecosystem and its complex balances as a whole,
required somewhat more time. Blanchan's writ-

ings, true to the sentiments of her time, had vilified some of the birds of prey. In her book *Birds Worth Knowing*, for example, she writes of Cooper's hawks, sharp-shinned hawks, and goshawks as "bloodthirsty villain[s] that live by plundering poultry yards, and tearing the warm flesh from the breasts of game and song birds. . . . [They] stab their cruel talons through the vitals of more valuable poultry, song and game birds, than any one would care to read about. . . . Let the guns be turned toward these bloodthirsty, audacious miscreants." Not for many years did nature books lose this moralistic and anthropomorphic tone. Not until the 1930s did the Audubon Society start to defend all predatory birds. It required several more decades for the budding discipline of ecology to convince the general public, along with those who determine national policy, that predators were neither useless nor evil animals worthy only of death but, rather, were integral parts of ecosystems and their balances and thus should not be eliminated. Scientists and authors such as Aldo Leopold encouraged a fundamental change in our concept of nature, and finally in 1972 the federal government ended its poisoning of predators.

Throughout the century, a plethora of environmental organizations and nature writers have continued to shape public opinion and policy in a major way. Another female author, Rachel

Carson, stands out as one of the most influential. Her publication of *Silent Spring* in 1962, which alerted the public to the dangers of environmental contaminants such as the synthetic pesticides, marked the beginning of the modern environmental movement. By the late 1960s, many viewed nature as a complex web within which all species play a part. This vision, along with the recognition of serious environmental degradation, set the groundwork for legislation to protect water and air, and for passage of the National Environmental Policy Act of 1970. This act coupled with establishment of the Environmental Protection Agency secured environmental protection as a national goal. The soon-to-follow Endangered Species Act, which called for concrete actions to preserve our nation's biodiversity, has played a major role in guiding rare bird species such as the bald eagle, whooping crane, and Kirtland's warbler away from extinction. Today the public demands that our government take strong steps to protect wildlife as well as the natural environment.

Thus in many ways today's scenario is far different from that of a century ago. Yet our bird populations continue to face numerous threats, some of which are far less evident and more difficult to address than those of the 1800s. We no longer fear the impact of market hunters, and sport hunting is now closely controlled. However, the demonstration of DDT's impact on eggshell thickness and hatchling rates of predatory birds has alerted us to the insidious potential impact of the synthetic chemicals that proliferate in modern times. Bird populations decline as birds deal with the dangers of windows, power lines, and tall buildings—threats that were far less numerous a century ago. Domestic and feral cats are a major problem, killing countless numbers of birds every year. Probably most significant, however, are the impacts of habitat fragmentation and destruction, fueled by the ever-greater demands of a growing human population on nature's resources. Year by year, these demands eliminate the North American nesting habitat of many songbirds. The spread of generalized species such as the brown-headed cowbird reduces the nesting success of many species, while others are displaced from their prime nesting habitat by range expansions of introduced species like the European starling. Neotropical migrants in their southerly wintering grounds face additional hazards from hunting, pesticides, and disappearing habitat.

Our nature writers persevere in educating us about these and other threats. Magazines and books, along with films, television, and the world wide web, bring us into daily contact with species and their problems around the world. Yet, while terms such as "biodiversity," "ecology," and "the balance of nature" have become common parlance, we may be no closer to comprehending nature's awesome complexity, integrity, and importance than we were a hundred years ago. At that time, in Blanchan's *Bird Neighbors*, John Burroughs expressed the following sentiments about the values of nature study fueled by nature guides:

> To add to the resources of one's life—think how much that means! To add to those things that make us more at home in the world; that help guard us against ennui and stagnation; that invest the country with new interest and enticement; that make every walk in the fields or woods an excursion into a land of unexhausted treasures; that make the returning seasons fill us with expectation and delight; that make every rod of ground like the page of a book in which new and strange things may be read; in short, those things that help keep us fresh and sane and young, and make us immune to the strife and fever of the world. The main thing is to feel an interest in Nature—an interest that leads to a loving unconscious study of her.

I think that both he and Blanchan would agree that today, as a century ago, we could benefit from a book on birds that every child (as well as every adult) *should* know, written with the hope, indeed with the trust, that the knowledge we gleaned from it would translate magically into meaningful action.

FURTHER READING

The history and impact of nature writing in this country are recorded in two enjoyable books, Paul Brooks's *Speaking for Nature* (Houghton Mifflin Company, Boston, 1980) and Frank Stewart's A *Natural History of Nature Writing* (Island Press, Washington, D.C., and Covelo, CA, 1995). A more specific examination of women nature writers in the early twentieth century is included in Carolyn Merchant's 1984 article, "Women of the Progressive Conservation Movement: 1900–1916" (*Environmental Review* 8: 57–85), and in Vera Norwood's *Made from This Earth: American Women and Nature* (University of North Carolina Press, Chapel Hill, 1993).

For a delightful look at Doubleday's model Country Life Press, see either of two publications entitled *Country Life Press*, published by Doubleday, Page and Company, Garden City, NY, in 1913 and 1919.

The National Audubon Society's story is recorded by Frank Graham, Jr., in *The Audubon Ark: A History of the National Audubon Society* (Alfred A. Knopf, NY, 1990). Robin Doughty takes a close look at the feather trade in *Feather Fashions and Bird Preservation: A Study in Nature Protection* (University of California Press, Berkeley, 1975).

The history of conservation in the United States has

been examined in numerous treatises. A few that were useful in preparing this essay are Thomas Dunlap's *Saving America's Wildlife: Ecology and the American Mind, 1850–1990* (Princeton University Press, Princeton, NJ, 1988) and Anthony Penna's *Nature's Bounty: Historical and Modern Environmental Perspectives* (M.E. Sharpe, Armonk, NY, 1999).

PREFACE

IF ALL his lessons were as joyful as learning to know the birds in the fields and woods, there would be no

> "   .   .   .   whining Schoole-boy with his Satchell
> And shining morning face creeping like Snaile
> Unwillingly to schoole."

Long before his nine o'clock headache appears, lessons have begun. Nature herself is the teacher who rouses him from his bed with an outburst of song under the window and sets his sleepy brain to wondering whether it was a robin's clear, ringing call that startled him from his dreams, or the chipping sparrow's wiry tremulo, or the gushing little wren's tripping cadenza. Interest in the birds trains the ear quite unconsciously. A keen, intelligent listener is rare, even among grown-ups, but a child who is becoming acquainted with the birds about him hears every sound and puzzles out its meaning with a cleverness that amazes those with ears who hear not. He responds to the first alarm note from the nesting blue birds in the orchard and dashes out of the house to chase away a prowling cat. He knows from afar the distress caws of a company of crows and away he goes to be sure that their persecutor is a hawk. A faint tattoo in the woods sends him climbing up a tall straight tree with the confident expectation of finding a woodpecker's nest within the hole in its side.

While training his ears, Nature is also training every muscle in his body, sending him on long tramps across the fields in pursuit of a new bird to be identified, making him run and jump fences and wade brooks and climb trees with the zest that produces an appetite like a saw-mill's and deep sleep at the close of a happy day.

When President Roosevelt was a boy he was far from strong, and his anxious father and mother naturally encouraged every interest that he showed in out-of-door pleasures. Among these, perhaps the keenest that he had was in birds. He knew the haunts of every species within a wide radius of his home and made a large collection of eggs and skins that he presented to the Smithsonian Museum when he could no longer endure the evidences of his "youthful indiscretion," as he termed the collector's mania. But those bird hunts that had kept him happily employed in the open air all day long, helped to make him the strong, manly man he is, whose wonderful physical endurance is not the least factor of his greatness. No one abhors the killing of birds and the robbing of nests more than he; few men, not spec-cialists, know so much about bird life.

Nature, the best teacher of us all, trains the child's eyes through study of the birds to quickness and precision, which are the first requisites for all intelligent observation in every field of knowledge. I know boys who can name a flock of ducks when they are mere specks twinkling in their rapid rush across the autumn sky; and girls who instantly recognise a gold-finch by its waving flight above the garden. The white band across the end of the kingbird's tail leads to his identification the minute some sharp young eyes perceive it. At a consider-able distance, a little girl I know distinguished a white-eyed from a red-eyed vireo, not by the colour of the iris of either bird's eye, but by the yellowish white bars on the white-eyed vireo's wings which she had noticed at a glance. An-other girl named the yellow-billed cuckoo, al-most hidden among the shrubbery, by the white thumb-nail spots on the quills of his out-spread tail where it protruded for a second from a mass of leaves. A little urchin from the New York City slums was the first to point out to his teacher, who had lived twenty years on a farm, the faint reddish streaks on the breast of a yellow warbler in Central Park. Many there are who have eyes and see not.

What does the study of birds do for the

imagination, that high power possessed by humans alone, that lifts them upward step by step into new realms of discovery and joy? If the thought of a tiny hummingbird, a mere atom in the universe, migrating from New England to Central America will not stimulate a child's imagination, then all the tales of fairies and giants and beautiful princesses and wicked witches will not cause his sluggish fancy to roam. Poetry and music, too, would fail to stir it out of the deadly commonplace.

Interest in bird life exercises the sympathies. The child reflects something of the joy of the oriole whose ecstasy of song from the elm on the lawn tells the whereabouts of a dangling "cup of felt" with its deeply hidden treasures. He takes to heart the tragedy of a robin's mud-plastered nest in the apple tree that was washed apart by a storm, and experiences something akin to remorse when he takes a mother bird from the jaws of his pet cat. He listens for the return of the bluebirds to the starch-box home he made for them on top of the grape arbour and is strangely excited and happy that bleak day in March when they re-appear. It is nature sympathy, the growth of the heart, not nature study, the training of the brain, that does most for us.

NELTJE BLANCHAN.

Mill Neck, 1906.

BIRDS EVERY CHILD SHOULD KNOW

CHAPTER I

OUR ROBIN GOODFELLOW AND HIS RELATIONS:

AMERICAN ROBIN
BLUEBIRD
WOOD THRUSH
WILSON'S THRUSH

THE AMERICAN ROBIN

Called also: Red-breasted Thrush; Migratory Thrush; Robin Redbreast

IT IS only when he is a baby that you could guess our robin is really a thrush, for then the dark speckles on his plump little yellowish-white breast are prominent thrush-like markings, which gradually fade, however, as he grows old enough to put on a brick-red vest like his father's.

The European Cock Robin—a bird as familiar to you as our own, no doubt, because it was he who was killed by the Sparrow with the bow and arrow, you well remember, and it was he who covered the poor Babes in the Wood with leaves—is much smaller than our robin, even smaller than a sparrow, and he is not a thrush at all. But this hero of the story books has a red breast, and the English colonists, who settled this country, named our big, cheerful, lusty bird neighbour a robin, simply because his red breast reminded them of the wee little bird at home that they had loved when they were children.

When our American robin comes out of the

turquoise blue egg that his devoted mother has warmed into life, he usually finds three or four baby brothers and sisters huddled within the grassy cradle. In April, both parents worked hard to prepare this home for them. Having brought coarse grasses, roots, and a few leaves or weed stalks for the foundation, and pellets of mud in their bills for the inner walls (which they cleverly managed to smooth into a bowl shape without a mason's trowel), and fine grasses for the lining of the nest, they saddled it on to the limb of an old apple tree. Robins prefer low-branching orchard or shade trees near our homes to the tall, straight shafts of the forest. Some have the courage to build among the vines or under the shelter of our piazzas. I know a pair of robins that reared a brood in a little clipped bay tree in a tub next to a front door, where people passed in and out continually. Doubtless very many birds would be glad of the shelter of our comfortable homes for theirs if they could only trust us. Is it not a shame that they cannot? Robins, especially, need a roof over their heads. When they foolishly saddle their nest on to an exposed limb of a tree, the first heavy rain is likely to soften the mud walls, and wash apart the heavy, bulky structure, when

"Down tumble babies and cradle and all."

It is wiser of them to fit the nest into the supporting crotch of a tree, as many do, and wisest to choose the top of a piazza pillar, where boys and girls and cats cannot climb to molest them, nor storms dissolve their mud-walled nursery. There are far too many tragedies of the nests after every heavy spring rain.

Suppose your appetite were so large that you were compelled to eat more than your weight of food every day, and suppose you had three or four brothers and sisters, just your own size, and just as ravenously hungry. These are the conditions in every normal robin family, so you can easily imagine how hard the father and mother birds must work to keep their fledglings' crops filled. No wonder robins like to live near our homes where the enriched land contains many fat grubs, and the smooth lawns, that they run across so lightly, make hunting for earth worms comparatively easy. It is estimated that about fourteen feet of worms (if placed end to end) are drawn out of the ground daily by a pair of robins with a nestful of babies to feed. When one of the parents alights near its home, every child must have seen the little heads, with wide-stretched, yellow bills, pop up suddenly like Jacks-in-the-box. How rudely the greedy babies push and jostle one another to get the most dinner, and how noisily they clamour for it! Earth worms are the staff of life to them just as bread is to children, but robins destroy vast quantities of other worms and insects more injurious to the farmers' crops, so that the strawberries and cherries they take in June should not be grudged them.

A man of science, who devoted many hours of study to learn the great variety of sounds made by common barnyard chickens in expressing their entire range of feeling, from the egg shell to the axe, could entertain an audience delightfully for an evening by imitating them. Similar study applied to robins would reveal as surprisingly rich results, but probably less funny. No bird that we have has so varied a repertoire as Robin Goodfellow, and I do not believe that any boy or girl alive could recognise him by every one of his calls and songs. His softly warbled salute to the sunrise differs from his lovely even-song just as widely as the rapturous melody of his courting days differs from the more subdued, tranquil love song to his brooding mate. Indignation, suspicion, fright, interrogation, peace of mind, hate, caution to take flight—these and a host of other thoughts, are expressed through his flexible voice.

Toward the end of June, you may see robins flying in flocks after sun-down. Old males and young birds of the first brood scatter themselves over the country by day to pick up the best living they can, but at night they collect in large numbers at some favourite roosting place. Oftentimes the weary mother birds are now raising second broods. We like to believe that the fathers return from the roosts at sun-up to help supply those insatiable babies with worms throughout the long day.

After family cares are over for the year, robins moult, and then they hide, mope, and keep silent for awhile. But in September, in a suit of new feathers, they are feeling vigorous and cheerful again; and, gathering in friendly flocks, they roam about the woodland borders to feed on the dogwood, choke cherries, juniper berries, and other small fruits. You see they change their diet with the season. By dropping the undigested berry seeds far and wide, they plant great numbers of trees and shrubs as they travel. Birds help to make the earth beautiful. With them every day is Arbour Day.

It is a very dreary time when the last robin leaves us, and an exceptionally cold winter when a few stragglers from the south-bound flocks do not remain in some sheltered, sunny, woodland hollow.

THE BLUEBIRD

Is there any sign of spring quite so welcome as the glint of the first bluebird unless it is his softly whistled song?   Before the farmer begins to plough the wet earth, often while the snow is still on the ground, this hardy little minstrel is making himself very much at home in our orchards and gardens while waiting for a mate to arrive from the South.

Now is the time to have ready on top of the grape arbour, or under the eaves of the barn, or nailed up in the apple tree, or set up on poles, the little one-roomed houses that bluebirds are only too happy to occupy.   More enjoyable neighbours it would be hard to find.   Sparrows will fight for the boxes, it is true, but if there are plenty to let, and the sparrows are persistently driven off, the bluebirds, which are a little larger though far less bold, quickly take possession.   Birds that come earliest in the season and feed on insects, before they have time to multiply, are of far greater value in the field, orchard, and garden than birds that delay their return until warm weather has brought forth countless swarms of insects far beyond the control of either bird or man.   Many birds would be of even greater service than they are if they received just a little encouragement to make their homes nearer ours.   They could save many more millions of dollars' worth of crops for the farmers than they do if they were properly protected while rearing their ever-hungry families.   As two or even three broods of bluebirds may be raised in a box each spring, and as insects are their most approved baby food, you see how much it is to our interest to set up nurseries for them near our homes.

But when people are not thoughtful enough to provide them before the first of March, the bluebirds hunt for a cavity in a fence rail, or a hole in some old tree, preferably in the orchard, shortly after their arrival, and proceed to line it with grass. From three to six pale blue eggs are laid. At first the babies are blind, helpless, and almost naked. Then they grow a suit of dark feathers with speckled, thrush-like vests similar to their cousin's, the baby robin's; and it is not until they are able to fly that the lovely deep blue shade gradually appears on their grayish upper parts. Then their throat, breast, and sides turn rusty red. While creatures are helpless, a prey for any enemy to pounce upon, Nature does not dress them conspicuously, you may be sure. Adult birds, that are able to look out for themselves, may be very gaily dressed, but their children must wear sombre clothes until they grow strong and wise.

Young bluebirds are far less wild and noisy than robins, but their very sharp little claws discourage handling. These pointed hooks on the ends of their toes help them to climb out of the tree hollow, that is their natural home, into the big world that their presence makes so cheerful.

As you might expect of creatures so heavenly in colour, the disposition of bluebirds is particularly angelic. Gentleness and amiability are expressed in their soft, musical voice. *Tru-al-ly, tru-al-ly*, they sweetly assert when we can scarcely believe that spring is here; and *tur-wee, tur-wee* they softly call in autumn when they go roaming through the country side in flocks of azure, or whirl through Southern woods to feed on the waxy berries of the mistletoe.

THE WOOD THRUSH

Called also: Song Thrush; Wood Robin; Bell Bird

Much more shy and reserved than the social, democratic robin is his cousin the wood thrush, whom, perhaps, you more frequently hear than see. Not that he is a recluse, like the hermit thrush, who hides his nest and lifts up his heavenly voice in deep, cool, forest solitudes; nor is he even so shy as Wilson's thrush, who prefers to live in low, wet, densely overgrown Northern woods. The wood thrush, as his name implies, certainly likes the woodland, but very often he chooses to stay close to our country and suburban homes or within city parks with a more than half-hearted determination to be friendly.

He is about two inches shorter than the robin. Above, his feathers are a rich cinnamon brown, brightest on his head and shoulders and shading into olive brown on his tail. His white throat and breast and sides are heavily marked with heart-shaped marks of very dark brown. He has a white eye ring.

"*Here am I*" come his three clear, bell-like notes of self-introduction. The quality of his music is delicious, rich, penetrative, pure and vibrating like notes struck upon a harp. If you don't already know this most neighbourly of the thrushes—as he is also the largest and brightest and most heavily spotted of them all— you will presently become acquainted with one of the finest songsters in America. Wait until evening when he sings at his best. *Nolee-a-e-o-lee-nolee-aeolee-lee!* peals his song from the trees. Love alone inspires his finest strains; but even in July, when bird music is quite inferior to that of May and June, he is still in good voice. A song so exquisite proves that the thrush comes near to being a bird angel, very high in the scale of development, and far, far beyond such low creatures as ducks and chickens.

Pit-pit-pit you may hear sharply, excitedly jerked out of some bird's throat, and you wonder if a note so disagreeable can really come from the wonderful songster on the branch above your head. By sharply striking two small stones together you can closely imitate this alarm call. Whom can he be scolding so severely? It is yourself, of course, for without knowing it you have come nearer to his low nest in the beech tree than he thinks quite safe. While sitting, the mother bird is, however, quite tame. A photographer I know placed his camera within four feet of a nest, changed the plates, and clicked the shutter three times for as many pictures without disturbing the gentle sitter who merely winked her eye at each chick.

Wood thrushes seem to delight in weaving bits of paper or rags into their deep cradles which otherwise resemble the robins.' A nest in the shrubbery near a bird-lover's home in New Jersey had many bits of newspaper attached to its outer walls, but the most conspicuous strip in front advertised in large letters "A House to be Let or Sold." The original builders happily took the next lease, and another lot of nervous, fidgety baby tenants came out of four light greenish-blue eggs; but, as usual, they moved away to the woods, aften ten days, to join the choir invisible.

WILSON'S THRUSH

The veery, as the Wilson's thrush is called in New England, is far more common there than the wood thrush, whose range is more southerly. During its spring and fall migrations only is it at all common about the elms and maples that men have planted. Take a good look at its tawny coat and lightly spotted cream buff breast before it goes away to hide. Like Kipling's "cat that walked by himself," the veery prefers the "wild, wet woods," and there its ringing, weird, whistling monotone, that is so melodious without being a melody, seems to come from you can't guess where. The singer keeps hidden in the dense, dark undergrowth. It is as if two voices, an alto and a soprano, were singing at the same time: *Whee-you, whee-you*: —the familiar notes might come from a scythe being sharpened on a whetstone, were the sound less musical than it is. The bird is too wise to sing very near its well-hidden nest, which is placed either directly on the damp ground or not far above it, and usually near water. Throughout its life the veery seems to show a distrust of us that, try as we may, few have ever overcome.

If you have thought that the thrush-like, cinnamon brown, speckle-breasted bird, with a long twitching tail like a catbird's, and a song as fine as a catbird's best, would be mentioned among the robin's relations, you must guess again, for he is the brown thrasher, not a thrush at all. You will find him in the Group of Lively Singers.

CHAPTER II

SOME NEIGHBOURLY ACROBATS

THE CHICKADEE

Called also: Black-capped Titmouse

BITTERLY cold and dreary though the day may be, that "little scrap of valour," the chickadee, keeps his spirits high until ours cannot but be cheered by the oft-repeated, clear, tinkling silvery notes that spell his name. *Chicka-dee-dee: chicka-dee-dee:* he introduces himself. How easy it would be for every child to know the birds if all would but sing out their names so clearly! Oh, don't you wish they would?

> "Piped a tiny voice near by
> Gay and polite—a cheerful cry—
> *Chick-chickadeedee!* Saucy note
> Out of sound heart and merry throat,
> As if it said, 'Good day, good Sir!
> Fine afternoon, old passenger!
> Happy to meet you in these places
> Where January brings few faces.'"

No bird, except the wren, is more cheerful than the chickadee, and his cheerfulness, fortunately, is just as "catching" as measels. None will respond more promptly to your whistle in imitation of his three very high, clear call notes, and come nearer and nearer to make quite sure you are only a harmless mimic. He is very inquisitive. Although not a bird may be in sight when you first whistle his call, nine chances out of ten there will be a faint echo from some far distant throat before very long; and by repeating the notes at short intervals you will have, probably, not one but several echoes from as many different chickadees whose curiosity to see you soon gets the better of their appetites and brings them flying, by easy stages, to the tree above your head. Where there is one chickadee there are apt to be more in the neighbourhood; for these sociable, active, cheerful little black-capped fellows in gray like to hunt for their living in loose scattered flocks throughout the fall and winter. When they come near enough, notice the pale rusty wash on the sides of their under parts which are more truly dirty white than gray. Chickadees are wonderfully tame: except the chipping sparrow, perhaps the tamest birds that we have. Patient people, who know how to whistle up these friendly sprites, can sometimes draw them close enough to touch, and an elect few, who have the special gift of winning a wild bird's confidence, can induce the chickadee to alight upon their hands.

Blessed with a thick coat of fat under his soft, fluffy gray feathers, a hardy constitution and a sunny disposition, what terrors has the winter for him? When the thermometer goes down, his spirits seem to go up the higher. Dangling like a circus acrobat on the cone of some tall pine tree; standing on an outstretched twig, then turning over and hanging with his black-capped head downward from the high trapeze; carefully inspecting the rough bark on the twigs for a fat grub or a nest of insect eggs, he is constantly hunting for food and singing grace between bites. His *day, day, day,* sung softly over and over again, seems to be his equivalent for "Give us this day our daily bread."

How delightfully he and his busy friends, who are always within call, punctuate the snow-muffled, mid-winter silence with their ringing calls of good cheer! The orchards where chickadees, titmice, nuthatches, and kinglets have dined all winter, will contain few worm-eaten apples next season. Here is a puzzle for your arithmetic class: If one chickadee eats four hundred and forty-four eggs of the apple tree moth on Monday, three hundred and thirty-three eggs of the canker worm on Tuesday, and seven hundred and seventy-seven miscellaneous grubs, larvæ, and insect eggs on Wednesday and Thursday, how long will it take a flock of twenty-two chickadees to rid an orchard of every unspeakable pest? One very wise and thrifty fruit grower I know attracts to his trees all the winter birds from far and near, by keeping on several shelves nailed up in his orchard, bits of suet, cheap raisins, raw peanuts chopped fine, cracked hickory nuts and rinds of pork. The free lunch counters are freely patronised. There is scarcely an hour in the day, no matter how cold, when some hungry feathered neighbour may not be seen helping himself to the heating, fattening food he needs to keep his blood warm.

At the approach of warm weather, chickadees retreat from public gaze to become temporary recluses in damp, deep woods or woodland swamps where insects are most plentiful. For a few months they give up their friendly flocking ways and live in pairs. Long journeys they do not undertake from the North when it is time to nest; but Southern birds move northward in the spring. Happily the chickadee may find a woodpecker's vacant hole in some hollow tree; worse luck if a new excavation must be made in a decayed birch—the favourite nursery. Wool from the sheep pasture, felt from fern fronds, bits of bark, moss, hair, and the fur of "little beasts of field and wood"—anything soft that may be picked up goes to line the hollow cradle in the tree-trunk. How the crowded chickadee babies must swelter in their bed of fur and feathers tucked inside a close, stuffy hole! Is it not strange that such hardy parents should coddle their children so?

TUFTED TITMOUSE

Called also: Peto Bird; Crested Tomtit; Crested Titmouse

Don't expect to meet the tufted titmouse if you live very far north of Washington. He is common only in the South and West.

This pert and lively cousin of the lovable little chickadee is not quite so friendly and far more noisy. *Peto-peto-peto* comes his loud, clear whistle from the woods and clearings where he and his large family are roving restlessly about all through the autumn and winter. A famous musician became insane because he heard one note ringing constantly in his overwrought brain. If you ever hear a troupe of titmice whistling *Peto* over and over again for hours at a time, you will pity poor Schumann and fear a similar fate for the birds. But they seem to delight in the two tiresome notes, uttered sometimes in one key, sometimes in another. Another call—*day-day-day*—reminds you of the chickadee's, only the tufted titmouse's voice is louder and a little hoarse, as it well might be from such constant use.

Few birds that we see about our homes wear a top knot on their heads. The big cardinal has a handsome red one, the larger blue jay's is bluish gray, the cedar waxwing's is a Quaker

drab; but the little titmouse, who is the size of
an English sparrow, may be named at once by
the gray pointed crest that makes him look so
pert and jaunty. When he hangs head downward from the trapeze on the oak tree, this
little gray acrobat's peaked cap seems to be
falling off; whereas the black skull cap on the
smaller chickadee fits close to his head no
matter how much he turns over the bar and
dangles.

Neither one of these cousins is a carpenter
like the woodpecker. The titmouse has a short,
stout bill without a chisel on it, which is why
it cannot chip out a hole for a nest in a tree
trunk or old stump unless the wood is much
decayed. You see why these birds are so
pleased to find a deserted woodpecker's hole.
Not alone are they saved the trouble of making
one, but a deep tunnel in a tree-trunk means
security for their babies against hawks, crows,
jays, and other foes, as well as against wind and
rain.

When you find a flock of either chickadees
or titmice, you may be sure it is made up chiefly,
if not entirely, of the birds of one or two broods
of the same parents. Their families are usually
large and the members devoted to one another.
Titmice nest in April so that you cannot tell the
brothers and sisters from the father and mother
when the troupe of acrobats leave the woods in

early autumn and whistle lustily about your
home.

WHITE-BREASTED NUTHATCH

Called also: Tree Mouse; Devil Downhead

When it comes to acrobatic performances in
the trees, neither the chickadee nor the titmouse can rival their relatives, the little bluish
gray nuthatches. Indeed, any circus might
be glad to secure their expert services. Hanging fearlessly from the topmost branches of the
tallest pine, running along the under side of
horizontal limbs as comfortably as along the
top of them, or descending the trunk head fore-
most, these wonderful little gymnasts keep their
nerves as cool as the thermometer in January.
From the way they travel over any part of the
tree they wish, from top and tip to the bottom
of it, no wonder they are sometimes called Tree
Mice. Only the fly that walks across the
ceiling, however, can compete with them in
clinging to the under side of boughs.

Why don't they fall off? If you ever have a
chance, examine their claws. These, you will
see, are very much curved and have sharp little
hooks that catch in any crack or rough place in
the bark and easily support the bird's weight.
As a general rule the chickadee keeps to the

end of the twigs and the smaller branches; the tufted titmouse rids the larger boughs of insects, eggs, and worms hidden in the scaly bark; but the nuthatches can climb to more inaccessible places. With the help of the hooks on their toes it does not matter to them whether they run upward, downward, or sidewise; and they can stretch their bodies away from their feet at some very queer angles. Their long bills penetrate into deep holes in the thick bark of the tree trunks and older limbs and bring forth from their hiding places insects that would escape almost every other bird except the brown creeper and the woodpecker. Of course, when you see any feathered acrobat performing in the trees, you know he is working hard to pick up a dinner, not exercising merely for fun.

The most familiar nuthatch, in the eastern United States, is the one with the white breast; but in the Northern States and Canada there is another common winter neighbour, a smaller compactly feathered, bluish gray gymnast with a pale rusty breast, a conspicuous black line running apparently through his eye from the base of his bill to the nape of his neck, and heavy white eyebrows. This is the hardy little red-breasted nuthatch. His voice is pitched rather high and his drawling notes seem to come from a lazy bird instead of one of the most vigorous and spry little creatures in the wood. The nasal *ank-ank* of his white-breasted cousin is uttered, too, without expression, as if the bird were compelled to make a sound once in a while against his will. Both of these cousins have similar habits. Both are a trifle smaller than the English sparrow. In summer they merely hide away in the woods to nest, for they are not migrants. It is only when nesting duties are over in the autumn that they become neighbourly.

Who gave them their queer name? A hatchet would be a rather clumsy tool for us to use in opening a nut, but these birds have a convenient, ever-ready one in their long, stout, sharply pointed bills with which they hack apart the small thin-shelled nuts like beech nuts and hazel nuts, chinquapins and chestnuts, kernels of corn and sunflower seeds. These they wedge into cracks in the bark just big enough to hold them. During the summer and early autumn when insects are plentiful, the nuthatches eat little else; and then they thriftily store away the other items on their bill of fare, squirrel fashion, so that when frost kills the insects, they may vary their diet of insect eggs and grubs with nuts and the larger grain. Flying to the spot where a nut has been securely wedged, perhaps weeks before, the bird scores and hacks and pecks it open with his sharp little hatchet, whose hard blows may be heard far away.

Although this tool is a great help to the nut-hatches in making their nests, they appear to be quite as ready to accept a deserted woodpecker's hole as the chickadee with a smaller bill. A natural cavity will answer, or, if they must, they will make one in some forest tree. The red-breasted nuthatches have a curious habit of smearing the entrance to the hole with fir-balsam or pitch. Why do you suppose they do it? Perhaps they think this will discourage egg suckers, like snakes, mice, or squirrels; but, in effect, the sticky gum often pulls the feathers from their own breasts as they go in and out attending to the wants of their family.

RUBY-CROWNED KINGLET

Count that a red-letter day on your calendar when first you see either this tiny, dainty sprite, or his next of kin, the golden-crowned kinglet, fluttering, twinkling about the evergreens. In republican America we don't often have the chance to meet two crowned heads. Energetic as wrens, restless as warblers, and as perpetually looking for insect food, the kinglets flit with a sudden, jerking motion from twig to twig among the trees and bushes, now on the lawn, now in the orchard and presently in the hedgerow down the lane. They have a pretty trick of lifting and flitting their wings every little while. The bluebird and pine grosbeak have it too, but their much larger, trembling wings seem far less nervous.

Happily the kinglets are not at all shy; no bird is that is hatched out so far north that it never sees a human being until it travels southward to spend the winter. Alas! It is the birds that know us too well that are often the most afraid. When the leaves are turning crimson and russet and gold in the autumn, keep a sharp look out for the plump little grayish, olive green birds that are even smaller than wrens, and not very much larger than hummingbirds. Although members of quite a different family—the kinglets are exclusive—they condescend to join the nuthatches and chickadees in the orchard to help clean the farmer's fruit trees or pick up a morsel at the free lunch counter in zero weather. Love or war is necessary to make the king show us his crown. But vanity or anger is sufficient excuse for lifting the dark feathers that nearly conceal the beauty spot on the top of his head when the midget's mind is at ease. If you approach very near—and he will allow you to almost touch him—you may see the little patch of brilliant red feathers, it is true, but you will probably get an unexpected, chattering scolding from the little king as he flies away.

In the spring his love song is as surprisingly strong in proportion to his size as the wren's. It seems impossible for such a volume of mellow flute-like melody to pour from a throat so tiny. Before we have a chance to hear it again the singer is off with his tiny queen to nest in some spruce tree beyond the Canadian border.

CHAPTER III

A GROUP OF LIVELY SINGERS

House Wren
Carolina Wren
Marsh Wren
Brown Thrasher
Catbird
Mockingbird

THE HOUSE WREN

IF YOU want some jolly little neighbours for the summer, invite the wrens to live near you year after year by putting up small, one-family box-houses under the eaves of the barn, the cow-shed, or the chicken-house, on the grape arbour or in the orchard. Beware of a pair of nesting wrens in a box nailed against a piazza post: they beat any alarm clock for arousing the family at sunrise.

Save the starch boxes, cover them with strips of bark, or give them two coats of paint to match the building they are to be nailed on. Cut a hole that you have marked on one end of each box by drawing a lead pencil around a silver quarter of a dollar. A larger hole would mean that English sparrows, who push themselves everywhere where not invited, would probably take possession of each house as fast as you nailed it up. Of course the little one-roomed cottages should have a number of small holes bored on the sides near the top to give the wrens plenty of fresh air. Have the boxes in place not later than the first of April—then watch. Would it not be a pity for any would-be tenants to pass by your home because they could

33

not find a house to let? Wrens really prefer
boxes to the holes in stumps and trees they
used to occupy before there were any white
people with thoughtful children on this continent. But the little tots have been known to
build in tin cans, coat pockets, old shoes, mit-
tens, hats, glass jars, and even inside a human
skull that a medical student hung out in the
sun to bleach!

When you are sound asleep some April morning, a tiny brown bird, just returned from a long
visit south of the Carolinas, will probably alight
on the perch in front of one of your boxes, peep
in the doorhole, enter—although his pert
little cocked-up-tail has to be lowered to let
him through—look about with approval, go
out, spring to the roof and pour out of his
wee throat a gushing torrent of music. The
song seems to bubble up faster than he can
sing. "Foive notes to wanst" was an Irishman's description of it. After the wren's
happy discovery of a place to live, his song will
go off in a series of musical explosions all day
long, now from the roof, now from the clothes-
posts, the fence, the barn, or the wood-pile.
There never was a more tireless, spirited, brilliant singer. From the intensity of his feelings,
he sometimes droops that expressive little tail
of his, which is usually so erect and saucy.

With characteristic energy, he frequently

begins to carry twigs into the house before he
finds a mate. The day little Jenny Wren
appears on the scene, how he does sing! Dashing off for more twigs, but stopping to sing to
her every other minute, he helps furnish the
cottage quickly, but, of course, he overdoes—
he carries in more twigs and hay and feathers
than the little house can hold, then pulls half
of them out again. Jenny gathers too, for she
is a bustling housewife and arranges matters
with neatness and despatch. Neither vermin
nor dirt will she tolerate within her well-kept
home. Everything she does to suit herself
pleases her ardent little lover. He applauds
her with song; he flies about after her with a
nervous desire to protect; he seems beside himself with happiness. Let any one pass too near
his best beloved, and he begins to chatter excitedly: "*Chit-chit-chit-chit*" as much as to
say, "Oh, do go away; go quickly! Can't you
see how nervous and fidgety you make me?"

If you fancy that Jenny Wren, who is
patiently sitting on the little pinkish chocolate
spotted eggs in the centre of her feather bed,
is a demure, angelic creature, you have never
seen her attack the sparrow, nearly twice her
size, that dares put his impudent head inside
her door. Oh, how she flies at him! How she
chatters and scolds! What a plucky little shrew
she is, after all! Her piercing, chattering, scold-

ing notes are fairly hissed into his ears until he
is thankful enough to escape.

THE LITTLE BROWN WREN*

There's a little brown wren that has built in our tree,
And she's scarcely as big as a big bumble-bee;
She has hollowed a house in the heart of a limb,
And made the walls tidy and made the floors trim
With the down of the crow's foot, with tow, and with straw
The cosiest dwelling that ever you saw.

This little brown wren has the brightest of eyes
And a foot of a very diminutive size.
Her tail is as trig as the sail of a ship.
She's demure, though she walks with a hop and a skip;
And her voice—but a flute were more fit than a pen
To tell of the voice of the little brown wren.

One morning Sir Sparrow came sauntering by
And cast on the wren's house an envious eye;
With a strut of bravado and toss of his head,
"I'll put in my claim here," the bold fellow said;
So straightway he mounted on impudent wing,
And entered the door without pausing to ring.

An instant—and swiftly that feathery knight
All towsled and tumbled, in terror took flight,
While there by the door on her favourite perch,
As neat as a lady just starting for church,
With this song on her lips, "He will not call again
Unless he is asked," sat the little brown wren.

If the bluebirds had her courage and hot,
quick temper, they would never let the sparrows
drive them away from their boxes. Unfortunately a hole large enough to admit a blue-

*From "Boy's Book of Rhyme," by Clinton Scollard

bird will easily admit those grasping monop-
olists; but Jenny Wren is safe, if she did but
know it, in her house with its tiny front door
It is amusing to see a sparrow try to work his
shoulders through the small hole of an empty
wren house, pushing and kicking madly, but
all in vain.

What rent do the wrens pay for their little
houses? No man is clever enough to estimate
the vast numbers of insects on your place that
they destroy. They eat nothing else, which is
the chief reason why they are so lively and
excitable. Unable to soar after flying insects
because of their short, round wings, they keep,
as a rule, rather close to the ground which their
finely barred brown feathers so closely match.
Whether hunting for grubs in the wood-pile,
scrambling over the brush heap after spiders,
searching among the trees to provide a dinner
for their large families, or creeping, like little
feathered mice, in queer nooks and crannies
among the outbuildings on the farm, they are
always busy in your interest which is also theirs.
It certainly pays, in every sense, to encourage
wrens.

THE CAROLINA WREN

The house wrens have a tiny cousin, a mite of
a bird, called the winter wren, that is so shy

and retiring you will probably never become well acquainted with it. It delights in mossy, rocky woods near running water. But a larger chestnut brown cousin, the Carolina wren, with a prominent white eyebrow, a bird which is quite common in the Middle and Southern States, sometimes nests in outbuildings and in all sorts of places about the farm. However, he too really prefers the forest undergrowths near water, fallen logs, half decayed stumps, and mossy rocks where insects lurk but cannot hide from his sharp, peering eyes. Now here, now there, appearing and disappearing, never at rest, even his expressive tail being in constant motion, he seems more nervously active than Jenny Wren's fidgety husband.

Some people call him the mocking wren, but I think he never deliberately tries to imitate other birds. Why should he? It is true that his loud-ringing, three-syllabled whistle, "*Tea ket-tle, Tea-ket-tle, Tea-ket-tle,*" suggests the crested titmouse's "*peto*" of two syllables, but in quality only; and some have thought that his whistled notes are difficult to distinguish from the one-syllabled, but oft-repeated, long-drawn *quoit* of the cardinal. These three birds are frequently to be heard in the same neighbourhood and you may easily compare their voices; but if you listen carefully, I think you will not accuse the wren of trying to mock either of the

others. In addition to his ringing, whistled
notes, he can make other sounds peculiarly his
own: trills and quavers, scolding *cacks*, rattling *kringggs*, something like the tree toad's, besides the joyful, lyrical melody that has given
him his reputation as a musician. Even these do
not complete his repertoire. To deliver his famous song, he chooses a conspicuous position in
the top of some bush or low tree; then, with
head uplifted and tail drooping—a favourite
posture of all these lively singers—he makes
us very glad indeed that we heard him. Happily he sings almost as many months in the
year as the most cheerful bird we have, the
song sparrow.

THE MARSH WREN

Hidden among the tall grasses and reeds along
the creeks and rivers, lives the long-billed marsh
wren, a nervous, active little creature that you
know at a glance. With tail cocked up and
even tilted forward toward her head in the ex-
treme of wren fashion, or suddenly jerked
downward to help keep her balance, she sways
with the grass as it blows in the wind—a dainty
little sprite. With no desire to make your
acquaintance, she flies with a short, jerky motion
(because of her short wings) a few rods away,

then drops into the grasses which engulf her as surely as if she had dropped into the sea. You may search in vain to find her now. Like the rails, she has her paths and runways among the tall sedges and cat-tails, where not even a boy in rubber boots may safely follow.

But she does not live alone. Withdraw, sit down quietly for awhile and wait for the excitement of your visit to subside; for every member of the wren colony, peering sharply at you through the grasses, was watching you long before you saw the first wren. Presently you hear a rippling, bubbling song from one of her neighbours; then another and another and still another from among the cat-tails which, you now suspect, conceal many musicians. The song goes off like a small explosion of melody whose force often carries the tiny singer up into the air. One explosion follows another, and between them there is much wren talk—a scolding chatter that is as great a relief to the birds' nervous energy as the exhaust from its safety valve is to a steam engine. The rising of a red-winged blackbird from his home in the sedges, the rattle of the kingfisher on his way up the creek, or the leisurely flapping of a bittern over the marshes is enough to start the chattering chorus.

Why are the birds so excited? This is their nesting season, May, and really they are too busy to be bothered by visitors. Most birds are content to make one nest a year but not these, who, in their excess of wren energy, keep on building nest after nest in the vicinity of the one preferred for their chocolate brown eggs. Bending down the tips of the rushes they somehow manage to weave them, with the weeds and grasses they bring, into a bulky ball suspended between the rushes and firmly attached to them. In one side of this green grassy globe they leave an entrance through which to carry the finer grasses for the lining and the down from last season's bursted cat-tails. When a nest is finished, its entrance is often cleverly concealed. If there are several feet of water below the high and dry cradle, so much the better, think the wrens—fewer enemies can get at them; but they do sometimes build in meadows that are merely damp. In such meadows the short-billed marsh wren, a slightly smaller sprite, prefers to live.

THE BROWN THRASHER

Called also: Brown Thrush; Long Thrush; Ground Thrush; Red Thrush; French Mocking-bird; Mavis.

People who are not very well acquainted with the birds about them usually mistake the

long-tailed brown thrasher for a thrush because
he has a rusty back and a speckled white breast,
which they seem to think is an exclusive thrush
characteristic, which it certainly is not. The
oven-bird and several members of the sparrow
tribe, among other birds, have speckled and
streaked breasts, too. The brown thrasher is
considerably larger than a thrush and his
habits are quite different. Watch him nervously twitch his long tail, or work it up
and down like one end of a see-saw, or suddenly jerk it up erect while he sits at attention
in the thicket, then droop it when, after mounting to a conspicuous perch, he lifts his head to
sing, and you will probably "guess right the
very first time" that he is a near relative of the
wrens, not a thrush at all. As a little sailor-
boy once said to me, "He carries his tell-tail
on the stern."

Like his cousin, the catbird, the brown thrasher
likes to live in bushy thickets overgrown with
vines. Here, running over the ground among
the fallen leaves, he picks up with his long slender bill, worms, May beetles and scores of other
kinds of insects that, but for him, would soon
find their way to the garden, orchard, and fields.
Yet few farmers ever thank him. Because
they don't often see him picking up the insects
in their cultivated land, they wrongly conclude
that he does them no benefit, only mischief,

because, occasionally, he does eat a little fruit. It seems to be a dreadful sin for a fellow in feathers to help himself to a strawberry or a cherry or a little grain now and then, although, having eaten quantities of insects that, but for him, would have destroyed them, who has earned a better right to a share of the profits?

Do you think the brown thrasher looks any more like a cuckoo than he does like a thrush? Simply because he is nearly as long as the dull brownish cuckoo and has a brown back, though of quite a different tawny shade, some boys and girls say it is difficult to tell the two birds apart. The cuckoo glides through the air as easily as if he were floating down stream, whereas the thrasher's flight, like the wren's, is tilting, uneven, flapping, and often jerky. If you make good use of your sharp eyes, you will be able to tell many birds by their flight alone, long before you can see the colour of their feathers. The passive cuckoo has no speckles on his light breast, and the yellow-billed cuckoo, at least, has white thumb-nail spots on his well-behaved tail, which he never thrashes, twitches, and balances as the active, suspicious thrasher does his. Moreover the cuckoo's notes sound like a tree-toad's rattle, while the thrasher's song—a merry peal of music —entrances every listener. He seems rather proud of it, to tell the truth, for although at

other times he may keep himself concealed
among the shrubbery, when about to sing, he
chooses a conspicuous perch as if to attract
attention to his truly brilliant performance.

The thrasher has been called a ground
"thrush" because it so often chooses to place
its nest at the roots of tall weeds in an open
field; but a low bush frequently suits it quite as
well. Its bulky nest is not a very choice piece
of architecture. Twigs, leaves, vine tendrils,
and bits of bark form its walls, and the speckled,
greenish blue eggs within are usually laid upon
a lining of fine black rootlets.

THE CATBIRD

Slim, lithe, elegant, dainty, the catbird, as
he runs lightly over the lawn or hunts among
the shrubbery, appears to be a fine gentleman
among his kind—a sort of Beau Brummel in
smooth, gray feathers who has preened and
prinked until his toilet is quite faultless. You
would not be surprised to hear that he slept
on rose petals and manicured his claws. He is
among the first to discover the bathing dish or
drinking pan that you have set up in your
garden, for he is not too squeamish, in spite of
his fine appearance, to drink from his bath.
With well-poised, black-capped head erect, and

tail up too, wren fashion, he stands at attention on the rim of the dish, alert, listening, tense— the neatest, trimmest figure in birddom.

After he has flown off to the nearest thicket, what a change suddenly comes over him! Can it be the same bird? With puffed out, ruffled feathers, hanging head, and drooping tail, he now suggests a fat, tousled schoolboy, just tumbled out of bed. Was ever a bird more contradictory? One minute, from the depths of the bushy undergrowth where he loves to hide, he delights you with the sweetest of songs, not loud like the brown thrasher's, but similar; only it is more exquisitely finished, and rippling. "*Prut! Prut! coquillicot!*" he begins. "*Really, really, coquillicot! Hey, coquillicot! Hey, victory!*" his inimitable song goes on like a rollicking recitative. The next minute you would gladly stop your ears when he utters the disagreeable cat-call that has given him his name. "*Zeay, Zeay*"—whines the petulant cry. Now you see him on the ground calmly looking for grass-hoppers, or daintily helping himself to a morsel from the dog's plate at the kitchen door. Suddenly, with a jerk and a jump, he has sprung into the air to seize a passing moth. There is always the pleasure of variety and the unexpected about the catbird.

He is very intelligent and friendly, like his cousin, the mockingbird. One catbird that comes to visit me at least ten times every day, can scarcely wait for the milk to be poured into the dog's bowl before he has flown to the brim for the first drink. Once, in his eagerness, he alighted on the pitcher in my hand. He has a pretty trick of flying to the sun dial as if he wished to learn the time of day. From this point of vantage, he will sail off suddenly, like a flycatcher, to seize an insect on the wing. He has a keen appetite for so many pests of the garden and orchard—moths, grasshoppers, beetles, caterpillars, spiders, flies and other insects—that his friendship, you see, is well worth cultivating. Five catbirds, whose diet was carefully watched by scientific men in Washington, ate thirty grasshoppers each for one meal.

Yet how many people ignorantly abuse the catbird! Because he has the good taste to like strawberries and cherries as well as we do, is he to be condemned on that account? If he kills insects for us every waking hour from April to October, don't you think he is entitled to a little fruit in June? The ox that treadeth out the corn is not to be muzzled, so that he cannot have a taste of it, you remember. A good way to protect our strawberry patches and cherry trees from catbirds, mockingbirds, and robins, is to provide fruit that they like much better— the red mulberry. Nothing attracts so many birds to a place. A mulberry tree in the chicken yard provides a very popular restaurant, not only for the song birds among the branches, but for the scratchers on the ground floor.

Like the yellow-breasted chat, the catbird likes to hide its nest in a tangle of cat brier along the roadside undergrowth and in bushy, woodland thickets. Last winter, when that vicious vine had lost every leaf, I counted in it eighteen catbird nests within a quarter of a mile along a country lane. Long before the first snowstorm, the inmates of those nests were enjoying summer weather again from the Gulf States to Panama. If one nest should be disturbed in May or June, when the birds are raising their families, all the catbird neighbours join in the outcry of mews and cat-calls. Should a disaster happen to the parents, the orphans will receive food and care from some devoted foster-mother until they are able to fly. You see catbirds are something far better than intelligent, musical dandies.

THE MOCKINGBIRD

What child is there who does not know the mockingbird, caged or free? In the North you very rarely see one now-a-days behind prison bars, for, happily, several enlightened states have made laws to punish people who keep our wild birds in cages or offer them for sale, dead or

alive.   When all the states make and enforce
similar laws, there will be an end to the barbaric
slaughter of many birds for no more worthy
end than the trimming of hats for thought-
less girls and women.   Birds of bright plumage
have suffered most, of course, but the mockingbirds' nests have been robbed for so many
generations to furnish caged fledglings for both
American and European bird dealers, that shot
guns could have done no work more deadly.
Where the people are too ignorant to understand
what mockingbirds are doing for them every day
in the year by eating insects in their gardens,
fields, parks, and public squares, they are shot
in great numbers for the sole offence of helping
themselves to a small fraction of the very fruit
they have helped to preserve.   Even the birds
ought to have a "square deal" in free America:
don't you think so?

Although not afflicted with "the fatal gift of
beauty," at least not the gaudy kind, like the
cardinal's and scarlet tanager's, the mockingbird's wonderful voice has brought upon him
an equal quantity of troubles.   Keenly intelligent though he is, he does not know enough to
mope and refuse to sing in a cage, but whiles
away the tedious hours of his captivity by all
manner of amusing and delightful sounds.   Indeed it has been found that the household pet is
apt to be a better mocker than the wild bird—

a most unfortunate discovery. Not only does he imitate the notes of birds about him, but he invents all manner of quips and vocal jugglery.

His love song is entrancing. "Oft in the stilly night," when the moonlight sheds a silvery radiance about every sleeping creature, the mockingbird sings to his mate such delicious music as only the European nightingale can rival. Perhaps the stillness of the hour, the beauty and fragrance of the place where the singer is hidden among the orange blossoms or magnolia, increase the magic of his almost pathetically sweet voice; but surely there is no lovelier sound in nature on this side of the sea. Our poet Lanier declared that this "heavenly bird" will be hailed as "Brother" by Beethoven and Keats when he enters the choir invisible in the spirit world.

Ever alert, on the *qui vive*, the mockingbird can no more suppress the music within him, night or day, than he can keep his nervous, high-strung body at rest. From his restlessness alone you might know he is the cousin of the catbird and brown thrasher and is closely related to the wrens. Flitting from perch to perch (fluttering is one of his chief amusements even in a cage), taking short flights from tree to tree, and so displaying the white signals on his wings and tail, hopping lightly, swiftly, gracefully over the ground, bounding into the air, or the next minute shooting his ashy gray body far across the garden and leaving a wake of music behind as he flies, he seems to be perpetually in motion. If you live in the South you can encourage no more delightful neighbour than this star performer in the group of lively singers.

CHAPTER IV

THE WARBLERS

YELLOW WARBLER

Called also: Summer Yellowbird; Wild Canary.

RATHER than live where the skies are gray and the air is cold, this adventurous little warbler will travel two thousand miles or more to follow the sun. A trip from Panama to Canada and back again within five months does not appal him. By living in perpetual sunshine his feathers seemed to have absorbed some of it, so that he looks like a stray sunbeam playing among the shrubbery on the lawn, the trees in the orchard, the bushes in the roadside thicket, the willows and alders beside the stream. He is shorter than the English sparrow by an inch. Although you may not get close enough to see that his yellow breast is finely streaked with reddish brown, you may know by these marks that he is not what you at first suspected he was—somebody's pet canary escaped from a cage. It is not he but the goldfinch—the yellow bird with the black wings—who sings like a canary. Happily he is so neighbourly that every child may easily become acquainted with this most common member of the large warbler family.

53

I don't believe there is anybody living who could name at sight every one of the seventy warblers that visit the United States. Some are very gaily coloured and exquisitely marked, as birds coming to us from the tropics have a right to be. Some are quietly clad; some, like the redstart, are dressed quite differently from their mates and young; others, like the yellow warbler, are so nearly alike that you could see no difference between the male and female from the distance of a few feet. Some live in the tops of evergreens and other tall trees; others, like the Maryland yellow-throat, which seems to prefer low trees and shrubbery, are rarely seen over twelve feet from the ground. A few, like the oven-bird, haunt the undergrowth in the woods or live most of the time on the earth. With three or four exceptions all the warblers dwell in woodlands, and it is only during the spring and autumn migrations that we have an opportunity to become acquainted with them; when they come about the orchard and shrubbery for a few days' rest and refreshment during their travels. Fortunately the cheerful little yellow warbler stays around our homes all summer long. Did you ever know a family so puzzling and contradictory as the Warblers?

The great majority of these fascinating and exasperating relatives are nervous, restless little sprites, constantly flitting from branch to branch and from twig to twig in a never-ending search for small insects. As well try to catch a weasel asleep as a warbler at rest. People who live in the tropics, even for a little while, soon become lazy. Not so the warblers, whose energy, like a steam engine's, seems to be increased by heat. Of course they do not undertake long journeys merely for pleasure, as wealthy human tourists do. They must migrate to find food; and as insects are most plentiful in warm weather, you see why these atoms of animation keep in perpetual motion. They are among the last migrants to come north in the spring and among the first to leave in the autumn because insects don't hatch out in cool weather, and the birds must always be sure of plenty to eat. Travelling as they do, chiefly by night, they are killed in numbers against the lighthouses and electric light towers which especially fascinate these poor little victims.

Who first misled us by calling these birds warblers? The truth is there is not one really fine singer, like a thrush, in the whole family. The yellow-breasted chat has remarkable vocal ability, but he is not a real musician like the mockingbird, who also likes to have fun with his voice. The warblers, as a rule, have weak, squeaky, or wiry songs and lisping *tseep* call notes, neither of which ought to be called a warble. The yellow warbler sings as acceptably as most of his kin. Seven times he rapidly repeats "*Sweet—sweet—sweet—sweet—sweet— sweeter-sweeter*" to his sweetheart, but this happy little lovemaker's incessant song is apt to become almost tiresome to everybody except his mate.

What a clever little creature she is! More than any other bird she suffers from the persecutions of that dusky rascal, the cowbird. In May, with much help from her mate, she builds an exquisite little cradle of silvery plant fibre, usually shreds of milkweed stalk, grass, leaves, and caterpillars' silk, neatly lined with hair, feathers, and the downy felt of fern fronds. The cradle is sometimes placed in the crotch of an elder bush, sometimes in a willow tree; preferably near water where insects are abundant, but often in a terminal branch of some orchard tree.

Scarcely is it finished before the skulking cowbird watches her chance to lay an egg in it that she may not be bothered with the care of her own baby. She knows that the yellow warbler is a gentle, amiable, devoted mother, who will probably work herself to death, if necessary, rather than let the big baby cowbird starve. But she sometimes makes a great mistake in her individual. Not all yellow warblers will permit the outrage. They prefer to weave a new bottom to their nest, over the cowbird's egg, although they may seal up their own speckled treasures with it. Suppose the wicked cowbird comes back and lays still another egg in the two-storied nest: what then? The little Spartan yellow bird has been known to weave still another layer of covering rather than hatch out an unwelcome, greedy interloper to crowd and starve her own precious babies. Two and even three-storied nests are to be found by bright-eyed boys and girls.

BLACK AND WHITE CREEPING WARBLER

You may possibly mistake this little warbler for a downy woodpecker when first you see him creeping rapidly over the bark of trees, or hanging from the under side of the branches. But when he flits restlessly from twig to twig and from tree to tree without taking time to examine spots thoroughly; especially when he calls a few thin wiry notes—*zee-zee-zee-zee*—you may know he is no woodpecker, but a warbler. Woodpeckers have thick set, high shouldered bodies which they flatten against the tree trunks; the males wear red in their caps, and all have larger, stouter bills than the warbler's. Moreover, no woodpecker is so small as this streaked and speckled little creature who is usually too intent on feeding to utter a single *zee*.   You could not possibly confuse him with the dilligent, placid brown creeper or with the slate-blue nuthatch which also creeps along the branches on the under or upper side.   Some children I know call this black and white warbler the little zebra bird.   Would that all warblers were so easily identified!

OVEN-BIRD

*Called also: The Teacher; Golden-crowned Thrush;
The Accentor.*

"Teacher—*Teacher*—ᴛᴇᴀᴄʜᴇʀ—TEACHER— TEACHER!" resounds a penetrating, accented voice from the woods.   Who calls?   Not an impatient scholar, as you might suppose, but a shy little thrush-like warbler who has no use whatever for any human being, especially at the nesting season in May and June, when he calls most loudly and frequently.   Beginning quite softly, he gradually increases the intensity of each pair of notes in a crescendo that seems to come from a point much nearer than it really does. Once heard it is never forgotten, and you can always be sure of naming at least one bird by his voice alone.   However, his really exquisite love song—a clear, ringing, vivacious melody, uttered while the singer is fluttering, hovering, high among the tree-tops—is rarely heard, or if heard is not recognised as the teacher's aerial serenade. He is a warbler, let it be recorded, who really can sing, and beautifully, however rarely.

Why is he called the oven-bird? A little girl I know was offered five dollars by her father if she could find the bird's nest in the high dry woods near her home. "*Teacher!*" was the commonest sound that came from them. It rang in her ears all day, so of course she thought it would be "too easy" to earn the money. Every afternoon, when school was out, she tramped through the woods hour after hour, poking about among the dead leaves, the snapping twigs, the velvety moss, the fallen logs, the young spring growth of the little plants and creepers, always keeping her eyes on the ground where she knew the nest would be found. Day after day she continued the search. Every time she saw a little hump of dead leaves or twigs and grasses her heart bounded with hope, but on closer examination she found no nest at all. Finally, one day when she was becoming discouraged, she spied in the path a little brownish olive bird, about the size of an English sparrow, but with a speckled, thrush-like breast and a dull orange V-shaped patch, bordered by black lines, on the top of his head. He was walking about on the ground, nodding his head as if

marking time, not hopping, sparrow-fashion;
and he took very dainty, pretty steps that suggested a French dancing master.   Occasionally
he would scratch the path for insects, like a tiny
chicken.   Although she had never seen the
teacher, and had expected that the loud voice
came from a much larger bird, she felt sure that
this must be he, so she sat down on a log and
watched and waited.   Presently she saw him tug
at a fine black hair-like root that lay across the
path, and, snapping it off, quickly fly away,
away—oh, where did he go with it?   She ran
stumbling after him through the undergrowth
to a little clearing.   There another bird, just
like him, whom she instantly guessed was his
mate, flew straight toward her, dropped to the
ground, ran about distractedly, dragging one
wing as if it were broken, and uttering sharp,
piteous notes of alarm.   The little girl didn't
like to distress the birds, of course, but how
could she resist the temptation to find their
nest?   So on she tramped around and around in
an ever widening circle, the excited birds still
hovering near and sharply scolding her.   You
may be sure she was quite as excited as they.

At last, a little dome-shaped mound of
grasses, half hidden among the dry brown oak
leaves and wild geranium, gladdened her eyes.
Running around to the opposite side she knelt
down on the grass, peeped under the arched roof

and into the nest, which was shaped like an old-fashioned Dutch oven. Was ever a sight so welcome? She almost screamed with joy. Through the opening on one side, that was about three inches high, she could see the lining of fine black rootlets, just like the one she had watched the bird snap off and carry away. Then she flew home, as if she too had wings, and, calling breathlessly "Oh Father! Father! I've found it!" burst into the house. A week before even one white speckled egg had been laid in the oven-bird's nest, there was a golden halfeagle in a happy little girl's palm. A fortnight later a man with a camera took a picture of the patient mother-bird, whose pretty striped head you see peeping out from under the dome.

MARYLAND YELLOW-THROAT

Called also: Black-masked Ground Warbler

This gay little warbler looks as if he were dressed for a masquerade ball with a gray-edged black mask over his face and the sides of his throat, a brownish green coat and a bright yellow vest. He is smaller than a sparrow. How sharply the inquisitive fellow peers at you through his mask whenever you pass the damp thicket, bordering the marshy land, where he likes best to live! And how quickly he hops from twig to twig and flies from one clump of bushes to another clump, in restless, warbler fashion, as he leads you a dance in pursuit! Not for a second does he stop watching you.

If you come too close, a sharp *pit-pit* or *chock* is snapped out by the excited bird, whose familiar, oft-repeated, sprightly, waltzing triplet has been too freely translated, he thinks, into, *Fol-low-me, fol-low-me, fol-low-me.* Pursuit is the last thing he really desires, and of course he issues no such invitation. What he actually says almost always sounds to me like *Witch-ee-tee, witch-ee-tee, witch-ee-tee.* You will surely hear him if you listen in his marshy retreats. He sings almost all summer. Except when nesting he comes into the garden, picks minute insects out of the blossoming shrubbery, hops about on the ground, visits the raspberry tangle, and hides among the bushes along the roadside. Only the yellow warbler, of all his numerous tribe, is disposed to be more neighbourly. In spite of his local name, he is to be found in winter from Georgia to Labrador and Manitoba westward to the Plains. You see he is something of a traveller.

The little bird who bewitches him, and to whom he sings the witch's song, wears no black mask, so it is not easy to name her if her mate is not about. Her plumage is duller than his and

the sides of her plump little body, which are
yellowish brown, shade into grayish white
underneath. Sometimes you may catch her
carrying weeds, strips of bark, broad grasses,
tendrils, reeds, and leaves for the outside of
her deep cradle, and finer grasses for its lining,
to a spot on the ground where plants and low
bushes help conceal it. She does not build so
beautiful a nest as the yellow warbler, but like
her she, too, poor thing, sometimes suffers
from the sneaking visits of the cowbird. Unhappily, she is not so clever as her cousin,
for she meekly consents to hatch out the cowbird's egg and let the big, greedy interloper
crowd and worry and starve her own brood.
Why does the cowardly cowbird always choose
a victim smaller than herself?

THE YELLOW-BREASTED CHAT

"Now he barks like a puppy, then quacks
like a duck, then rattles like a kingfisher, then
squalls like a fox, then caws like a crow, then
mews like a cat—*C-r-r-r-r-r-whrr*-that's it—
Chee-quack,   cluck,   yit-yit-yit-now—hit   it—
*tr-r-r-r-wheu-caw-caw-cut, cut-tea-boy-who, who-
mew, mew,*" writes John Burroughs of this
rollicking polyglot, the chat; but not even
that close student of nature could set down on

paper all the multitude of queer sounds with which the bird amuses himself. He might be mistaken for a dozen different birds and animals in as many minutes.

Such a secretive roysterer is he that you may rarely see him, however often you may hear his voice when he is hidden beyond sight in partial clearings or the bushy, briery, thickety openings in the woods. As he seems to delight in keeping pursuers off by a natural fence of barbed wire, the cat brier, wild blackberry, raspberry, and rose bushes are among his favourite plants. But if you will sit down quietly near his home, your patience will probably be rewarded by the sight of this largest of the warblers, with olive green upper parts, a conspicuous white line running from his bill around his eye and another along his throat, and a bright yellow breast shading to grayish white underneath. He is over an inch longer than the English sparrow. His wife looks just like him.

The zany at the circus can go through no more clownish tricks than the chat. See him, a mere bunch of feathers, dance and balance in the air, now fluttering, now falling as if he had been shot, or turning aerial somersaults, now rising and trailing his legs behind him like a stork, now dropping out of sight in the thickest part of the thicket. The instant he spies you, *Chut-chut*, he scolds from the briars. Shy, eccentric, absurd, but inspired with a "fine frenzy," which is a passionate love for his mate and their nest, all his queer notes and equally queer stunts centre about his home. On moonlight nights, Punchinello entertains himself and Columbine with a series of inimitable performances which have earned him the title of yellow mockingbird. He can throw his voice so that it seems to come from quite a different direction, as you may sometime have heard a human ventriloquist do.

THE REDSTART

When this exquisite little warbler flashes his brilliant salmon flame and black feathers among the trees, darting hither and thither, fluttering, spinning about in the air after insects caught chiefly on the wing, you will surely agree that he is the most beautiful as well as the most lively bird in the woods. The colour scheme of his clothes suggests the Baltimore oriole's, only the flaming feathers on the sides of his body, wings, and tail are a pinker shade of flame, and the black ones which cover his back, throat, and upper breast, are more glossy, with bluish reflections. Underneath he is white, tinged with salmon. But you could not possibly mistake this lovely little sprite for the oriole, he is so much smaller—about an inch shorter than the sparrow. His cousin, the Blackburnian warbler, a much rarer bird, with a colour scheme of black, white, and beautiful rich orange, not salmon flame, can be named instantly by the large amount of white in his tail feathers. There are so few brilliantly coloured birds that find their way to us from the tropics, that it should not take any boy or girl longer to learn them than it does to learn the first multiplication table. In Cuba the redstart is known as "El Candelita"—the little candle flame that flashes in the deep, dark, tropical forest.

Who would believe that this small firebrand, half glowing, half charred, whirling about through the trees, as if blown by the wind, is a cousin of the sombre oven-bird that walks so daintily and leisurely over the ground? The redstart keeps perpetually in motion that he may seize gnats and other gauzy winged mouthfuls in mid-air—not as the flycatchers do, by waiting on a fence rail or limb of a tree for a dinner to fly past, then dashing out and seizing it, but by flitting about constantly in search of insect prey. The bristles at the base of his bill prevent many an insect from getting past it. He rests on the trees only long enough to snatch a morsel, then away he goes again. No wonder the Spaniards call all the gaily coloured, tropical wood warblers "Mariposas"—butterflies.

CHAPTER V

THE VIREOS:
ANOTHER STRICTLY AMERICAN FAMILY

RED-EYED VIREO
WHITE-EYED VIREO
YELLOW-THROATED VIREO
WARBLING VIREO

THE VIREOS

YOU know that if the birds should suddenly perish, there wouldn't be a leaf, a blade of grass, or any green thing left upon the earth within a few years—it would be uninhabitable.

When Dame Nature, the most thorough of housekeepers, gave to the birds the task of restraining insects within bounds so that man and beast could live, she gave the care of foliage to the vireos. It is true that most of the warblers, and a few other birds too, hunt for their food among the leaves, but with nothing like the vireo's painstaking care and thoroughness. The nervous, restless warblers flit from twig to twig without half exploring the foliage; whereas the deliberate, methodical vireos search leisurely above and below it, cocking their little heads so as to look up at the under side of the leaf above them and to peck off the destroyers hidden there—bugs of many kinds and countless little worms, caterpillars, weevils, inchworms, May beetles, and leaf-eating beetles. Singing as they go, no birds more successfully combine work and play.

Because they spend their lives among the foliage, the vireos are protectively coloured; with soft grayish or olive green on their backs, wings, and tail, whitish or yellow below. Some people call them greenlets. They are all a little smaller than sparrows. More inconspicuous birds it would be hard to find or more abundant, although so commonly overlooked except by people on the look-out for them. Where the new growth of foliage at the ends of the branches is young and tender, many insects prefer to lay their eggs that their babies may have the most dainty fare as soon as they are hatched. They do not reckon upon the vireos' visits.

Toward the end of April or the first of May, these tireless gleaners return to us from Central and South America where they have spent the winter, which of course you know, is no winter on the other side of the equator, but a continuation of summer for them. Competition for food being more fierce in the tropics than it is here, millions of birds besides the warblers and vireos travel from beyond the Isthmus of Panama to the United States and back again every year in order that they may live in perpetual summer with an abundance of food. If any child thinks that birds are mere creatures of pleasure, who sing to pass the time away, he doesn't begin to understand how hard they must work for a living. They cannot limit their labours to an eight-hour day. However, they keep cheerful through at least sixteen busy hours.

THE RED-EYED VIREO

Almost everywhere in the Eastern United States and Canada, the red-eyed vireo is the most common member of his family. The only individual touch to his costume that helps to distinguish him is a gray cap edged with a black line which runs parallel to his conspicuous white eyebrow. He wears a dull olive coat and a white vest. But listen to the Preacher! You have no need to meet him face to face in order to know him: "*You see it—you know it—do you hear me?—do you believe it?*" he propounds incessantly through the long summer days, even after most other birds are silent. You cannot mistake his voice. With a rising inflection at the end of each short, jerky sentence, he asks a question very distinctly and sweetly, then pauses an instant as if waiting for a reply—an unusually courteous orator. His monotonous monologue, repeated over and over again, comes to us from the elms and maples in the village street, the orchard and woodland, where he keeps steadily and deliberately at work. Some boys say they can whittle better if they whistle. Vireos seem to hunt more thoroughly if they sing.

Like the rest of his kin, the red-eyed vireo is quite tame. A little girl I know actually stroked the pretty head of a mother bird as she sat brooding in her exquisite nest, and a week later carried one of the young birds all around the garden on a rake handle.

Vireos are remarkably fine builders—among the very best. Although their nests are not so deep as the Baltimore orioles', the shape and weave are similar. The red-eye usually prefers to swing her cradle from a small crotch in an oak or apple tree or sapling, and securely lace it through the rim on to the forked twigs. Nests vary in appearance, but you will notice that these weavers show a preference for dried grass as a foundation into which are wrought bits of bark, lichen, wasps' nest "paper," spider web, plant down, and curly vine tendrils.

THE WHITE-EYED VIREO

It is not often that you can get close enough to any bird to see the white of his eyes, but the brighter olive green of this vivacious little white-eyed vireo's upper parts, his white breast, faintly washed with yellow on the sides, and the two yellowish white bars on his wings help you to recognise him at a distance. Imagine my surprise to meet him in Bermuda, over six hundred miles out at sea from the Carolina coast, where he, too, was taking a winter vacation! In those beautiful islands, where our familiar catbirds and cardinals also abound, the white-eyed vireo is the most common bird to be seen. His sweet, vigorous, irregular interrogation may be heard all day. But there he is known by quite a different name—"Chick of the Village." It was a pleasant shock to hear, "*Now, who are you, eh?*" piquantly sung out at me, a stranger in the islands, by this old acquaintance in a hibiscus bush within a few steps of the pier where the steamer landed.

In the United States where he nests, his manners are less sociable; in fact they are rather pert, even churlish at times, and never very friendly. Here he loves to hide in such low, briery, bushy tangles as the chat and catbird choose. By no stretch of the imagination would his *chic* Bermuda name fit him here, for he has little to do with villages and he resents your advances toward more intimate acquaintance with harsh, cackling scoldings, half to himself, half to you, until you, in turn, resent his impertinence and leave him alone— just what the independent little fellow wanted. He has a strong, decided character, you perceive.

His precious nest, so jealously guarded, is a deeper cup than that of his cousin with the red eye, deeper than that of any of the other vireos, and it usually contains three favourite materials in addition to those generally chosen by them: they are bits of wood usually stolen from some woodpecker's hole, shreds of paper.

and yards and yards of fine caterpillar silk,
by which the nest is hung from its slender fork
in the thicket. It also contains, not infre-
quently, alas! a cowbird's most unwelcome egg.

THE YELLOW-THROATED VIREO

In a family not conspicuous for its fine
feathers, this is certainly the beauty. The
clear lemon yellow worn at its throat spreads
over its vest; its coat is a richer and more
yellowish green than the other vireos wear, and
its two white wing-bars are as conspicuous as
the white-eyed vireo's. Moreover its mellow
and rich voice, like a contralto's, is raised to
a higher pitch at the end of a sweetly sung
triplet. "*See me; I'm here; where are you?*" the
singer inquires over and over again from the
trees in the woodland, or perhaps in the village
when nesting duties are not engrossing. Don't
mistake it for the chat simply because its
throat is yellow.

As this is the beauty of the family, so is it
also the best nest builder.

THE WARBLING VIREO

High up in the top of elms and maples that
line village streets where the red-eyed vireo loves

to hunt, even among the trees of so busy a thoroughfare as Boston Common, an almost continuous warble in the early summer indicates that some unseen singer is hidden there; but even if you get a glimpse of the warbling vireo you could not tell him from his red-eyed cousin at that height. Modestly dressed, without even a white eye-brow or wing-bars to relieve his plain dusty olive and whitish clothes, he is the least impressive member of his retiring, inconspicuous family. He asks you no questions in jerky, colloquial triplets of song, so you may know by his voice at least that he is not the red-eyed vireo. Some self-conscious birds, like the song sparrow, mount to a conspicuous perch before they begin to sing, as if they had to deliver a distinct number on a programme before a waiting audience. Not so with this industrious little gleaner to whom singing and dining seem to be a part of the same performance—one and inseparable. He sings as he goes, snatching a bit of insect food between warbles.

Although towns do not affright him, he really prefers wooded border-land and clearings, especially where birch trees abound, when it is time to rear a family.

CHAPTER VI

BIRDS NOT OF A FEATHER

THE BUTCHER-BIRDS OR SHRIKES

IS IT not curious that among our so-called song birds there should be two, about the size of robins, the loggerhead and the northern shrike, with the hawk-like habit of killing little birds and mice, and the squirrel's and blue jay's trick of storing what they cannot eat? They are butchers, with the thrifty custom of hanging up their meat, which only improves in flavour and tenderness after a day or two of curing. Then, even if storms should drive their little prey to shelter and snow should cover the fields, they need not worry nor starve seeing an abundance in their larder provided for the proverbial rainy day.

In the Southern and Middle States, where the smaller loggerhead shrike is most common, some children say he looks like a mockingbird; but the feathers on his back are surely quite a different gray, a light-bluish ash, and pearly on his under parts, with white in his black wings and tail which is conspicuous as he flies. His powerful head, which is large for his size, has a heavy black line running from the end of his mouth across his cheek, and his strong bill has a hook on the end which is useful in tearing the flesh from his victim's bones.   He really looks like nothing but just what he is—a butcher-bird.

See him, quiet and preoccupied, perched on a telegraph pole on the lookout for a dinner! A kingbird, or other flycatcher which chooses similar perches, would sail off suddenly into the air if a winged insect hove in sight, snap it up, make an aerial loop in its flight and return to its old place.   Not so the solitary, sanguinary shrike.   When his wonderfully keen eyes detect a grasshopper, a cricket, a big beetle, a lizard, a little mouse, or a sparrow at a distance in a field, he drops like an eagle upon the victim, seizes it with his strong beak, and flies with steady flapping strokes of the wings, close along the ground, straight to the nearest honey locust or spiny thorn; then rises with a sudden upward turn into the tree to impale his prey.   Hawks, who use the same method of procuring food, have very strong feet; their talons are of great help in holding and killing their victims; but the shrikes, which have rather weak, sparrow-like feet, for perching only, are really compelled in many cases to make use of stout thorns or sharp twigs to help them quiet the struggles of their victims.   Weather-vanes, lightning rods, bare branches, or the outermost or top branches of tall trees, high poles, and telegraph wires, which afford a fine bird's eye-view of the surrounding hunting ground, are favourite points of vantage for both shrikes. When it is time to husk the corn, every farmer's boy must have seen a shrike sitting on a fence-rail or hovering in the air ready to seize the little meadow mice that escape from the shocks.

It is sad to record that sometimes shrikes also sneak upon their prey. When they resort to this mean method of securing a dinner they leave the high perches and secrete themselves in clumps of bushes in the open field. Luring little birds within striking distance by imitating their call notes, they pounce upon a terror-striken sparrow before you could say "Jack Robinson." Shrikes seem to be the only creatures that really rejoice in the rapid increase of English sparrows. In summer they prefer large insects, especially grasshoppers, but in winter when they can get none, they must have the fresh meat of birds or mice. At any season they deserve the fullest protection for the service they do the farmer. Shrikes kill only that they themselves may live, and not for the sake of slaughter, which is a so-called sport reserved for man alone, who in any case, should be the last creature to condemn them.

The loggerhead's call-notes are harsh, creaking, and unpleasant, but at the approach of the nesting season he proves that he really can sing, although not half as well as his cousin, the northern shrike, who astonishes us with a fine

song some morning in early spring.   Before we
become familiar with it, however, the wandering minstrel is off to the far north to nest within
the arctic circle.   It is only in winter that the
northern shrike visits the United States, travelling as far south as Virginia and Kansas between
October and April.   He is larger than the loggerhead, being a little over ten inches long, a
goodlooking winter visitor in a gray suit with
black and white trimmings on his wings and tail
and wavy bars on his breast.   Bradford Torrey
used to visit a vireo that would drink water
from a teaspoon which he held out to her while
she sat brooding on her nest.   I know a lady
who fed bits of raw meat to a wounded shrike
from the tines of a fork, the best substitute
for a thorn she could find, because he found it
awkward to eat from a dish.

THE CEDAR WAXWING

*Called also: Cedarbird; Cherry-bird; Bonnet
bird, Silk-tail.*

So few birds wear their head feathers crested
that it is a simple matter to name them by
their top-knots alone, even if you did not see
the gray plumage of the little tufted titmouse,
the dusky hue of the crested flycatcher, the blue

of the jay and the kingfisher, the red of the cardinal, and the richly shaded grayish-brown of the cedar waxwing, which is, perhaps, the most familiar of them all. His neat and well-groomed plumage is fine and very silky, almost dove-like in colouring, and although there are no gaudy features about it, few of our birds are so exquisitely dressed. The pointed crest, which rises and falls to express every passing emotion, and the velvety black chin, forehead, and line running apparently through the eye, give distinction to the head. The tail has a narrow yellow band across its end, and on the wings are the small red spots like sealing wax that are responsible for the bird's queer name. The waxwing is larger than a sparrow and smaller than a robin.

But it is difficult to think of a single bird when one usually sees a flock. Sociable to a degree, the waxwings rove about a neighbourhood in scattered companies, large and small, to feed on the cedar or juniper berries, chokecherries, dog-wood and woodbine berries, elder, haw, and other small wild fruits on which they feed very greedily; then move on to some other place where their favourite fruit abounds. Happily, they care very little about our cultivated fruit and rarely touch it. A good way to invite many kinds of birds to visit one's neighbourhood is to plant plenty of berry-bearing trees and shrubs.   The birds themselves plant most of the wild ones, by dropping the undigested berry seeds far and wide.   How could the seeds of many species be distributed over thousands of miles of land without their help?   If will surprise you to count the number of trees about your home that have been planted, quite unconsciously, by birds many years before you were born.   Cedarbirds are responsible for no small part of the beauty of the lanes and hedgerows throughout their wide range from sea to sea and from Canada to Mexico and Central America.   Nature, you see, makes her creatures work for her, whether they know they are helping her plans or not.

When a flock of cedarbirds enters your neighbourhood, there is no noisy warning of their coming.   Gentle, refined in manners, courteous to one another, almost silent visitors, they will sit for hours nearly motionless in a tree while digesting a recent feast.   An occasional bird may shift his position, then, politely settling himself again without disturbing the rest of the company, remain quiet as before. Lisping, *Twee-twee-zee* call notes, like a hushed whispered whistle, are the only sounds the visitors make.   How different from a roving flock of screaming, boisterous blue jays!

When rising to take wing, the squad still keeps together, flying evenly and swiftly in close ranks on a level with the tree-tops along a straight course; or, wheeling suddenly, the birds dive downward into a promising, leafy, restaurant. Enormous numbers of insects are consumed by a flock. The elm-beetle, which destroys the beauty, if not the life, of some of our finest shade trees, would be exterminated if there were cedarbirds enough. One flock within a week rid a New England village of this pest that had eaten the leaves on the double row of elms which had been the glory of its broad main street for over a hundred years. When you see these birds in an orchard, look for better apples there next year. Canker-worms are a *bon bouche* to them; so are grubs and caterpillars, especially cutworms.

Sometime after all the other birds, except the tardy little goldfinch, have nested, the waxwings give up the flocking habit and live in pairs. Toward the end of June, when many birds are rearing the second brood, you may see a couple begin to carry grass, shreds of bark, twine, fine roots, catkins, moss or rags—any or all of these building materials—to some tree, usually a fruit tree or a cedar; and then, if you watch carefully, you will find what is not always the case with humans—the birds' manners at home are even better than when moving in society abroad. The devoted male brings dainties to his brooding mate and helps her feed

their family. Moreover, cedarbirds are very
good to feathered orphans.

THE SCARLET TANAGER

Called also: Black-winged Redbird

People who are now living can remember
when scarlet tanagers were as common as robins.
Where are they now? You see a redbird at
the north so rarely that a thrill of excitement is
felt when a flash of scarlet among the tree-tops
makes the day a red-letter one on your bird
calendar. Alas! He has, what has certainly
proved to be, the fatal gift of beauty. A
scarlet coat with black wings and tail, worn by
a bird larger than a sparrow, makes a shining
mark among the foliage for the shot gun and
sling shot. Thousands of tanagers have been
slaughtered to be worn on the unthinking heads
of vain girls and women. Many are killed
every year, during the spring and autumn
migrations, by flying against the great lighthouses along our coasts, the birds' highway
of travel. Tanagers, who are only summer
visitors from the tropics, are peculiarly suscepti-
ble to cold; a sudden change in the weather,
a drop in the thermometer some time in May
just after they have come here from a warmer

climate and are still especially sensitive, will kill off great numbers in the north woods and in Canada. They really should postpone their journey a little while until the weather becomes settled and there are fewer fogs on the coast.

The male tanager, in his wedding garment, is sometimes mistaken for a cardinal by people who only half see any object they look at. Bird study sharpens the sight wonderfully, and teaches boys and girls the importance of accurrate observation. The cardinal, a larger bird, is almost as large as a robin; he is a rich, deep red all over, and not a scarlet shade. Moreover he wears a pointed crest by which you may always know him, while the tanager, whose head is smooth, may be certainly named by his black wings and tail. After the nesting season, the tanager begins to moult and then he is a queer looking object indeed in his motley coat. Only little patches and streaks of scarlet remain here and there among the olive green feathers that gradually replace the red ones until, in winter, he becomes completely transformed into an olive bird with black wings, looking like his immature sons. How tiresome to have to change his feathers again toward spring before he can hope to woo and win a mate!

The exacting little lady bird, who demands such fine feathers, is herself quietly clad in light olive green with a more yellowish tinge on her

lighter breast that she may be in perfect colour
harmony with the leaves she lives and nests
among. If she, too, wore scarlet, I fear the
tanager tribe would have disappeared years
ago. Happily her protective colouring, which
betrays no nest secrets, has saved the species.

Is it not strange that birds, who spend the
rest of their lives among the tree-tops, hunting
among the foliage for insects and small fruit,
should nest so low? Sometimes they place
their cradle on a limb only six feet from the
ground. It is a rather shabby, poorly made
affair which very lively tanager youngster might
easily tumble apart. "*Chip—churr*" calls the
gorgeous father from the tree top, and a re-
assuring reply that all is well with the nest
floats up to him from his mate. He does not
often risk its safety by showing himself near
the nest, securely hidden by the foliage below.
If, toward the end of May, you hear him singing
his real song, which is somewhat like an oriole's
mellow, cheery carol, you may be sure he is
planning to spend the summer in your neighbourhood. Not many miles from New York
there is a house built on the top of a hill, whose
sides are covered with oak and chestnut woods,
where one may be sure to see tanagers among
the tree tops from any window at any hour of
any day from May to October. Several nests
in those woods are saddled on to the horizontal

limbs of the white oak. Not many people are blessed with such beautiful, interesting neighbours.

In the Southern States, one of the most familiar birds in the orange groves, orchards, and woods of pine and oak, is the summer tanager, another smooth-headed redbird, but without a black feather on him. He is fire red all over. Of the three hundred and fifty species of tanagers in the tropics, only two think it worth while to visit the Eastern United States and one of these frequently suffers because he starts too early. Suppose all should suddenly decide to come north some spring and spend the summer with us! Our woods would be filled with some of the most brilliant and gorgeous birds in the world. Don't you wish all the members of the family were as adventurous as the scarlet tanager?

CHAPTER VII

THE SWALLOWS

THE SWALLOWS

IF YOU were a bird, could you think of any way of earning a living more delightful than sailing about in the air all day, playing cross-tag on the wing with your companions, skimming low across the meadows, ponds and marshes, or rising high above them and darting hither and thither wherever you pleased, without knowing what it means to feel tired? Swallows are as much in their element when in the air as fish are in water; but don't imagine they are there simply for fun. Their long, blade-like wings, which cut the air with such easy, but powerful strokes, propel them enormous distances before they have collected enough mosquitoes, gnats and other little gauzy-winged insects to supply such great energy and satisfy their hunger. With mouth widely gaping, leaving an opening in the front of their broad heads that stretches from ear to ear, they get a tremendous draught down their little throats, but they gather in a dinner piece-meal just as the chimney swift, whip-poor-will and night-hawk do. Viscid saliva in the bird's mouth glues the little victims as fast as if they were caught on sticky fly-paper; then, when

enough have been trapped to make a pellet, the
swallow swallows them in a ball, although
one swallow does not make a dinner, any more
than one swallow makes a summer.

These sociable birds delight to live in companies, even during the nesting season when
most feathered couples, however glad to flock
at other times, prefer to be alone. As soon as
the young birds can take wing, one family
party unites with another, one colony with
another, until often enormous numbers assemble
in the marshes in August and September. You
see them strung like beads along the telegraph
wires, perched on the fences, circling over the
meadows and ponds, zigzagging across the
sky. Millions of swallows have been noted in
some of these autumnal flocks. Usually they
go to sleep among the reeds and grasses in a
favourite marsh where the bands return year
after year; but some prefer trees. Comparatively
little perching is done except at night, for swallows' feet are very small and weak.

At sunrise, the birds scatter in small bands
to pick up on the wing the long continued meal,
which lasts till late in the afternoon. Those
who have gone too far abroad and must travel
back to the roost after sundown shoot across
the sky with incredible swiftness lest darkness
overtake them. Relying upon their speed of
flight to carry them beyond the reach of en-

emies, they migrate boldly by daylight instead of at night as the timid little vireos and warblers do. During every day the swallows are with us they must consume billions and trillions of blood-sucking insects that would pester other animals beside ourselves. Think of the mosquito bites alone that they prevent! Every one of us is greatly in their debt.

Male and female swallows are dressed so nearly alike that you can scarcely tell one from the other. Both twitter merrily but neither really sings.

THE PURPLE MARTIN

There is a picturesque old inn beside a post road in New Jersey with a five-storied martin house set up on a pole above its quaint swinging sign. For over thirty years a record was kept on the pole showing the dates of the coming and going of the martins in April and September, which did not vary by more than two or three days during all that time. The inn-keeper locked up in his safe every night the registers on which were entered the arrivals and departures of his human guests, but he valued far more the record of his bird visitors which interested everybody who stopped at his inn.

One day, while he was away, a man who was painting a fence for him thought he would surprise him by freshening up the old, weather-beaten pole. Alas! He painted over every precious mark. You may be sure the surprise recoiled upon him like a boomerang when the wrathful inn-keeper returned. However, the martins continue to come back to their old home year after year and rear their broods on little heaps of leaves in every room in the house, which is the cheerful fact of the story.

These glossy, blue-black iridescent swallows, grayish white underneath, the largest of their graceful tribe, have always been great favourites. Even the Indians in the Southern States used to hang gourds for them to nest in about their camps—a practice continued by the Negroes around their cabins to this day. Strangely enough these birds which nested and slept in hollow trees before the coming of the white men, were among the first to take advantage of his presence. Now, in the Eastern United States, at least, the pampered darlings of luxury positively refuse to live where people do not put up houses for their comfort. In the sparsely settled West, however, they still condescend to live in trees, but only when they must, like the chimney-swifts, who, by the way are no relation. Plenty of people persist in calling them chimney swallows, which is precisely what they are not. Not even the little house wren has adapted itself so quickly to civilised men's homes, as the swift and purple martin.

Intelligent people, who are only just beginning to realise what birds do for us and how very much more they might be induced to do, are putting up boxes for the martins, not only near their own houses, that the birds may rid the air of mosquitoes, but in their gardens and orchards that incalculable numbers of injurious pests in the winged stage may be destroyed. When martins return to us in spring from Central and South America, where they have passed the winter, insects are just beginning to fly, and if they can be captured then, before they have a chance to lay their eggs, you see how much trouble and money are saved for the farmers by their tireless allies, the swallows. Unfortunately, purple martins are not so common at the North as they were before the coming of those saucy little immigrants, the English sparrows, who take possession, by fair means or by foul, of every house that they can find. In the South, where the martins are still very numerous, a peach grower I know has set up in his orchard rows of poles, with a house on each, either for them or for bluebirds. He says these bird partners are of inestimable value in keeping his fruit trees free from insects.

The curculio, one of the worst enemies every fruit grower has to fight, destroying as it does millions of dollars worth of crops every year, is practically unknown in that Georgia planter's orchard. Some day farmers all over the United States will wake up and copy his good idea.

A colony of martins circling about a house give it a delightful home-like air. Their very soft, sweet conversation with one another as they fly, sounds like rippling, musical laughter.

THE BARN SWALLOW

Do you know where there is an old-fashioned, weather-worn barn, with its hospitable doors standing open, where you could not find at least one pair of barn swallows at home beneath its roof? These birds, you will notice, prefer dilapidated old farm buildings, whose doors are off their hinges, and whose loose shingles or broken clapboards offer plenty of entrances and exits. If you like to play around a barn as well as every child I know, you must be already acquainted with the exquisite, dark steel-blue swallows with glistening reddish buff breasts, and deeply forked tails, that dart and glide in and out of the openings, merrily twittering as they fly. While you tumble about in the hay among the rafters the swallows go and come, so that, quite unconsciously, you will associate them with happy hours as long as you live.

High up on some beam, too high for the children to reach, let us hope, a pair of barn swallows will plaster their mud cradle. Did you ever see them gathering pellets of wet soil in their bills at some roadside puddle? It is, perhaps, the only time you can ever catch them with their feet on the earth. Each mud pill must be carried to the barn and fastened on to the rafter. Countless trips are made to the puddle before a sufficient number of pellets are worked into the deep mud walls of the ample nursery. Usually grass is mixed with the mud, but some swallows make their bricks without straw. A lining of fine hay and plenty of feathers from the chicken yard seem to be essential for their comfort, which is a pity, because almost always chicken feathers are infested with lice, and lice kill more young birds than we like to think about. When there is a nestful of fledglings to feed, sticky little pellets of insects, caught on the wing, are carried to them by both parents from daylight to dusk. Do notice how tirelessly they work!

In a family famous for graceful, rapid flight, the barn swallow easily excels all his relations. The deep fork in his tail enables him to steer himself with those marvellously quick, erratic turns, which make his course through the air resemble forked lightning. But with what exquisite grace he can also glide and skim across the water, fields and meadows without an apparent movement of the wing! His flight seems the very poetry of motion. The ease of it accounts for the very wide distribution of barn swallows from southern Brazil in winter to Greenland and Alaska in summer. What a journey to take twice a year!

THE EAVE OR CLIFF SWALLOW

More than any other bird family, the swallows are becoming increasingly dependent for shelter upon man, at least when they are nesting; and as this is the season when they are most valuable to him because of the enormous numbers of insects they prevent from multiplying, let us hope that familiarity with us will never breed contempt and cause them to return to their old, uncivilised building sites. In the sparsely settled West, the cliff swallow still fastens its queer, gourd-shaped, mud nest against projecting rocks, but in the East it is so quick to take advantage of the eaves of the barns and other out-buildings, that its old name does not apply, and we know it here only as an eave swallow.

The barn swallow, as we have seen, chooses to nest upon the rafters inside the barn, but the eave swallow is content to stay outside under the shelter of a projecting roof. In such a place you find not one, but several or many mud tenements plastered in a row against the wall, for eave swallows are always remarkably sociable, even at the nesting season. A photograph of a colony I have seen shows one hundred and fifteen nests nearly all of which touch one another.

Although so often noticed circling about barns, you may know by the rusty patch on the lower part of his steel-blue back, the crescent-shaped white mark on his forehead, and the notched, not deeply forked tail, that the eave swallow is not the barn swallow, which it otherwise resembles.

THE BANK SWALLOW

Called also: Sand Martin; Sand Swallow

Perhaps you have seen a sand bank somewhere, probably near a river or pond, where the side of the bank was filled with holes as if a small cannon had been trained against it as a target. In and out of the holes fly the smallest of the swallows, with no lovely metallic blue or glistening buff in their dull plumage, which is plain brownish gray above, white underneath, with a grayish band across the breast. Only their cousin, the rough-winged swallow, whose breast is brownish gray, is so plainly dressed.

The giggling twitter of the bank swallows as they wheel and dart through the air above you, proves that they are never too busy hunting for a dinner to speak a cheerful word to their friends. Year after year a colony will return to a favourite bank, whose face has been honeycombed with such care. Think of the labour and patience required for so small a bird to dig a tunnel two feet deep, more or less! Some nests have been placed as far as four feet from the entrance. You are not surprised at the big kingfisher, who also tunnels a hole in a bank for his family, because his long, strong bill makes digging comparatively easy; but for the small-billed, weak-footed swallow, the work must be difficult indeed. What a pity they cannot hire moles to make the tunnels with their strong, flat, spade-like feet. No wonder the birds become attached to the tunnels that have cost so much labour. When there are no longer any baby swallows on the heaps of twigs, grass and feathers at the end of them, the birds use them as resting places by day as well as by night until it is time to gather in vast flocks and speed away to the tropics.

THE TREE SWALLOW

Called also: White-breasted Swallow

Probably this is the most abundant swallow that we have; certainly countless numbers assemble every year in the Long Island and Jersey marshes, perch on the telegraph wires and skim, with much circling, above the meadows and streams in a perfect ecstasy of flight. At a little distance the bird appears to be black above and white below, but as he suddenly wheels past, you see that his coat is a lustrous dark steel green. Immature birds are brownish gray. All have white breasts.

As the tree swallows are the only members of their family who spend the winter in the Southeastern United States, they can easily arrive at the North some time before their relatives from the tropics overtake them. And they are the last to leave. Myriads remain in the vicinity of New York until the middle of October. There is plenty of time to rear two broods, which accounts for the great size of the flocks. By the Fourth of July the young of the first broods are off hunting for little gauzy-winged insects over the low lands; and about a month later the parents join their flock, bringing with them more youngsters than you could count. They sleep every night in the marshes, clinging to the reeds,

Like the cliff swallow, the tree swallow is fast losing the right to its name. It takes so kindly to the boxes we set up for martins, bluebirds and wrens that, where sparrows do not interfere, it now prefers them to the hollow trees, which once were its only shelter. But some tree swallows still cling to old-fashioned ways and at least rest in hollow trees and stumps, even if they do not nest in them. Some day they may become as dependent upon us as the martins and, like them, refuse to nest where boxes are not provided.

CHAPTER VIII

THE SPARROW TRIBE

Song Sparrow
Swamp Sparrow
Field Sparrow
Vesper Sparrow
English Sparrow
Chipping Sparrow
Tree Sparrow
White-throated Sparrow
Fox Sparrow
Junco
Snowflake
Goldfinch
Purple Finch
Indigo Bunting
Towhee
Rose-breasted Grosbeak
Cardinal Grosbeak

THE SPARROW TRIBE

L IKE the poor, the sparrows are always with us. There is not a day in the year when you cannot find at least one member of the great tribe which comprises one-seventh of all our birds—by far the largest North American family. What is the secret of their triumphant numbers?

Many members of the hardy, prolific clan, wearing dull brown and gray-streaked feathers, in perfect colour harmony with the grassy, bushy places or dusty roadsides where they live, are usually overlooked by enemies in search of a dinner. Undoubtedly their protective colouring has much to do with their increase. They are small birds mostly, not one so large as a robin.

Sparrows being seed eaters chiefly, although none of the tribe refuses insect meat in season, and all give it to their nestlings, there is never a time when they cannot find food, even at the frozen North where some weedy stalks project above the snow. They are not fastidious. Fussy birds, like fussy people, have a hard time in this world; but the whole sparrow tribe, with few exceptions, make the best of things as they find them and readily adapt themselves to whatever conditions they meet. How wonderfully that saucy little gamin, the English sparrow, has adjusted himself to this new land!

Members of the more aristocratic finch and grosbeak branches of the family, however, who wear brighter clothes, pay the penalty by decreasing numbers as our boasted civilisation surrounds them. Gay feathers afford a shining mark. Naturally grosbeaks prefer to live among protective trees. They are delightful singers, and so, indeed, are some of their plain little sparrow cousins.

All the members of the family have strong, conical bills well suited to crush seeds, and gizzards, like a chicken's, to grind them fine. These little grist-mills within the birds' bodies extract all the nourishment there is from the seed. The sparrow tribe, you will notice, do immense service by destroying the seeds of weeds, which, but for them, would quickly overrun the farmer's fields and choke his crops. Because these hardy gleaners can pick up a living almost anywhere, they do not need to make very long journeys every spring and autumn. Their migrations are comparatively short when undertaken at all. As a rule their flight is laboured, slow, and rather heavy—just the opposite from the wonderfully swift and graceful flight of the swallows.

THE SONG SPARROW

This is most children's favourite bird: is it yours? Although by no means the belle of the family, the song sparrow is beloved throughout its vast range if for no other reason than because it is irrepressibly cheerful. Good spirits are contagious: every one feels better for having a neighbour always in a good humour. Most birds mope when it rains, or when they shed their feathers, or when the weather is cold and dreary, or when something doesn't please them, and cultivate their voices only when they fall in love in the happy spring-time. But you may hear the hardy, healthful song sparrow's " merry cheer" almost every month in the year, in fair weather or in foul, in the middle of the night and in broad daylight, when a little mate is to be wooed with light-hearted vivacity, when two, three, or even four broods severely tax the singer's energy through the summer, when clothes must be changed in August and when the cold of approaching winter drives every other singer from the choir. The most familiar song—for this tuneful sparrow has at least six similar but slightly different melodies in his repertoire—begins with a full round note three times repeated, then dashes off into a sweet, short, lively, intricate strain that almost trips itself in its hasty utterance. Few people whistle well enough to imitate it. Few birds can rival the musical ecstacy.

Artlessly self-confident, not at all bashful, the song sparrow mounts to a conspicuous perch when he sings, rather than let his efforts be muffled by foliage. Don't mistake him for an English sparrow; notice his distinguishing marks: the fine dark streaks on his light breast tend to form a larger blotch in the centre. You see him singing on the extended branch of some low tree, on the topmost twig of a bush, on a fence, or a piazza railing from which he dives downward into the grass, or flies straight along into the bushes, his tail working like a pump handle as if to help his flight. Very rarely he flies upward. Diving into a bush is one of his specialties. He best likes to live in regions near water.

The song sparrows that come almost every day in the year among many other birds to my piazza roof for waste canary seed and such delicacies, show refreshing spirit in driving off the English sparrows who, let it be recorded, can get not a morsel until the song sparrows are abundantly satisfied. One of the latter is quite able to keep off half a dozen of his English cousins. How does he do it? Not by his superior size, for the measurements of both birds show that they are about the same length although the song sparrow's slightly longer and more graceful tail makes him appear a trifle larger. Certainly not by any rowdy, bold assaults, which are the English bird's specialty. But by simply assuming superiority and expressing it only by running in a threatening attitude toward each English sparrow who dares to alight on the roof, does he bluff him into flying away again! There is never a fight, not even an ill-mannered scolding, just quiet monopoly for a few minutes, then a joyous outburst of song. After that the English sparrows may take the songster's leavings.

SWAMP SPARROW

Where rails thread their way among the rushes, and red-winged blackbirds, marsh wrens, and Maryland yellow-throats like to live, there listen for the *tweet-tweet-tweet* of the swamp sparrow. It is a sweet but rather monotonous little song that he repeats over and over again to the mate who is busy about her grassy nest in a tussock not far away, but well hidden among the rank swamp growth.

Some children say it is difficult to tell the plain gray-breasted swamp sparrow from the larger song sparrow with the streaked breast; but I am sure their eyes are not so sharp as yours.

FIELD SPARROW

While the neighbourly song sparrow and the swamp sparrow delight to be near water, the field sparrow chooses to live in dry uplands where stunted bushes and cedars cover the hills and overgrown old fields, and towhees and brown thrashers keep him company. He is not fond of human society, however, and usually flies away with wavering, uncertain flight from bush to bush rather than submit to a close scrutiny of his bright chestnut brown back and crown, flesh-coloured bill, gray eyebrow, grayish throat, buffy breast and light feet. Because his tail is a trifle longer than the chippy's he is slightly larger than the smallest of our sparrows. Unless you notice that his bill is not black and his head not marked with black and gray streaks like the chippy's, you might easily mistake him for his sociable, confiding little cousin who comes hopping to the door.

How differently he sings! Listen for him some evening after sunset when his simple vesper hymn, clear, plaintive, sweet, rings from the bush where he perches especially for the performance. Scarcely any two field sparrows sing precisely alike. Most of them, however, begin with three clear, smooth, leisurely whistles—*cher-wee, cher-wee, cher-wee*—then hurry through the other notes—*cheo, cheo-dee-dee-eee, e, e—*

which run rapidly into a trill before they die away. Others reverse the time and diminish the measures toward the close. However sung, the song, which makes the uplands tuneful all day and every day from April to August, does not vary its quality, which is as fine as the vesper sparrow's.

Hatched in a bush, and almost never seen apart from one, this humble little bird might well be called the bush sparrow.

VESPER SPARROW

To name this little dingy sparrow that haunts the open fields and dusty roadsides, you must notice the white feather on each side of his tail as he spreads it and flies before you to alight upon a fence. Like the song sparrow, this cousin has some fine dark streaks on his throat and breast. If you get near enough you will notice that his wing coverts, which are a bright chestnut brown, make the rest of his sparrow plumage look particularly pale and dull. Some people call him the bay-winged bunting; others, the grass finch, because he nests, like the meadow-lark and many other foolish birds, on the ground where mice, snakes, mowing machines and cats often make sad havoc of his young family.

The field sparrow, as we have seen, prefers neglected old fields overgrown with bushes, but the vesper sparrow chooses more broad, open, breezy, grassy country. When busy picking up insects and seed on the ground, he takes no time for singing, but keeps steadily at work, unlike the vireos that sing between bites. With him music is a momentous matter to which he is quite willing to devote half an hour at a time. He usually mounts to a fence rail or a tree before beginning the repetitions of his lovely, serene vesper which is most likely to be heard about sunset, or at sunrise, if you are not a sleepy-head. Like the rose-breasted grosbeak, he has the delightful habit of singing through the early hours of the summer night.

ENGLISH SPARROW

Is there a boy or girl in America who does not already know this saucy, keen-witted little gamin who thrives where other birds would starve; who insists upon thrusting himself where he is not wanted, not only in other bird's houses, but about the cornices, pillars, and shutters of our own, where his noise and dirt drive good housekeepers frantic; who, without any weapons but his boldness and impudence to fight with, fears neither man nor beast, and who multiplies as fast as the rabbit, so that he is rapidly inheriting the earth? Even children who have never been out of the slums know at least this one bird, this ever-present nuisance, for he chirps and chatters as cheerfully in the reeking gutters as in the prettiest gardens; he hops with equal calm about the horse's feet and trolley cars in crowded city thoroughfares, as he does about flowery fields and quiet country lanes; he will pick at the overflow from garbage pails on the sidewalk in front of teeming tenements and manure on the city pavements with quite as much relish as he will eat the fresh clean seed spilled by a canary, or cake-crumbs from my lady's hand. Intense cold he endures with cheerful fortitude and as intense mid-summer heat without losing his astonishing vitality. Is it any wonder that a bird so readily adaptable to all sorts of conditions should thrive like a weed and beat his way around the world?

Now that he has gained such headway in this country his extermination is practically impossible, since a single pair of sparrows might have 275,716,983,698 descendants in ten years! It is foolish to talk of ridding the land of these vermin of birddom. The conditions that kept them in check at home are lacking in this great land of freedom and so we Americans must pay the penalty for ignorantly tampering with nature.

Sparrows were first imported into Brooklyn in 1851 to rid the shade trees of inch worms. This feat they accomplished there and in New York with neatness and despatch. Every one fed, petted, and coddled them then. It was not until many years later that their true character came to be thoroughly understood. Then it was found by scientific men in Washington, after the fairest trial any culprits ever received, that not all the insects and weed seeds they destroy compensate for the damage they do in the farmer's grain fields, to say nothing of their harrassing and dispossessing other birds more desirable. But they kill no birds, so we may hope that, in the course of time, our native songsters may pluck up courage to claim their rights and hold their own, learning from the sparrows the important lesson of adaptability.

CHIPPING SPARROW

Called also: Chippy; Door-step Sparrow; Hair Sparrow.

This summer a pair of the sociable, friendly little chippies—the smallest members of their clan—decided that they would build in a little boxwood tree on the verandah of our house next to the front door through which members of the family passed every hour of the day. While we sat within a few feet of the tree, both birds would carry into it fine twigs and grasses for the foundation of the nest and, later, long horse hairs which they coiled around and around to form a lining. Where did they get so many hairs? A few might have been switched out of the horses' tails in the stable yard or dropped on the road, but what amazingly bright eyes the birds must have to find them, and how curious that chippies alone, of all the feathered tribe, should always insist upon using them to line their cradles!

From the back of a settle, the round of a rocking chair, or the gnomon of the sun-dial near the verandah, the little chippy would trill his wiry tremulo, like the locust's hot weather warning, while his mate brooded over five tiny greenish-blue eggs in the boxwood tree. Before even the robin was awake, earlier than dawn, he would start the morning chorus with the simple little trill that answers for a song to express every emotion throughout the long day. Both he and his mate use a *chip* call note in talking to each other.

When she was tired brooding, of which she did far more than her share, he would relieve her while she went in search of food. Very often he would carry to the nest a cabbage worm for her or some other refreshing delicacy. The screen door might bang beside her while she sat

close upon her treasures without causing her
to do more than flutter an eye-lid. Every
member of the family parted the twigs of boxwood that enclosed the nest to look upon her
pretty little reddish-brown head with a gray
stripe over the eye and a dark-brown line running apparently through it. All of us gently
stroked her from time to time. She would
occasionally leave the nest for only a minute or
two to pick up the crumbs, chickweed, and
canary seed scattered for her about the verandah floor, and showed not the slightest fear
when we went on with our regular occupations.
We were the breathlessly excited ones, while
she hopped calmly about our feet. The chippy
is wonderfully tame—perhaps the tamest bird
that we have.

You may be sure there was joy in the household when the nest in the boxwood contained
baby chippies one morning—not a trace of egg-
shells which had been carried away early.
Insects were the only approved baby-food and
we were greatly astonished to see what large
ones were thrust down the tiny, gaping throats
every few minutes. Instead of flying straight
to the nest, both parents would frequently stop
to rest or get proper direction on the back or
the arm of a chair where some one was sitting.
In eight days the babies began to explore the
verandah. Then they left us suddenly without

a "good-bye." No guests whom we ever had beneath our roof left a more aching void than that chipping sparrow family. How we hope they will find their way back to the boxwood tree from the Gulf States next April!

TREE SPARROW

Called also: Winter Chippy

When the friendly little chippy leaves us in autumn, this similar but larger sparrow cousin comes into the United States from the North, and some people say they cannot tell the two birds apart or the field sparrow from either of them. The tree sparrow, which, unlike the chippy, has no black on his forehead, wears an indistinct black spot on the centre of his breast where the chippy is plain gray, and the field sparrow is buffy. The tree sparrow has a parti-coloured bill, the upper-half black, the lower yellow with a black tip, while the chippy has an entirely black bill, and the field sparrow a flesh-coloured or pale-red one. Only the tree sparrow, which is larger than either of the others, although only as large as a full grown English sparrow, spends the winter in the Northern United States, and by that time his confusing relatives are too far south for comparison. It is in spring and autumn that their ranges over-lap and there is any possibility of confusion.

When the slate-coloured juncos come from their nesting grounds far over the Canadian border, look also for flocks of tree sparrows in fields and door yards, where crab grass, amaranth and fox tail grass, among other pestiferous weeds, are most abundant. I do not know how Professor Beal of the Department of Agriculture, arrived at his conclusions, but he estimates that in a single state—Iowa— the tree sparrows alone destroy eight hundred and seventy-five tons of noxious weed seeds every winter. Then how incalculably great must be our debt to the entire sparrow tribe!

Tree sparrows welcome other winter birds to their friendly flocks that glean a comfortable living from the weed stalks protruding from the snow. Their cheerful, soft, jingling notes have been likened by Mr. Chapman to " sparkling frost crystals turned to music."

WHITE-THROATED SPARROW

Called also: Peabody-bird; Canada Sparrow

"What's in a name?" Our English cousins over the border are quite sure they hear this sparrow sing the praises of *Swee-e-et Can-a-da*, *Can-a-da*, *Can-a-da-ah*, while the New Englanders think the bird distinctly says, *I-I-Pea-body, Pea-bod-y, Pea-bod-y-I*, extolling the name of one of their first families. You may amuse yourself by fitting whatever words you like to the well-marked metre of the clear, high-pitched, plaintive, sweet song of twelve notes. Learn to imitate it and you will be able to whistle up any white-throat within reach of your voice in the Adirondacks, the White Mountains, or the deep, cool woods of Maine, throughout the summer, although the majority of these hardy sparrows nest on the northern side of the Canadian border. Our hot weather they cannot abide. When there is a keen breath of frost in the air and the hedgerows and thickets in the United States are taking on glorious autumnal tints, listen for the white-throated migrants conversing with sharp *chink* call-notes that sound like the ring of a marble-cutter's chisel.

During the autumn and spring migrations, when these birds are likely to give us the semi-annual pleasure of coming closer about our homes, with other members of their sociable tribe, you will see that the white-throat is a slightly larger and more distinguished bird than the English sparrow, and that he wears a white patch above his plain, gray breast. Except the white-crowned sparrow, who wears a black and white-striped soldier cap on his head, and who sometimes travels in migrating flocks with his cousins, the white-throated sparrow is the handsomest member of his plain tribe.

FOX SPARROW

Do you imagine because he is called the fox sparrow that this bird has four legs, or that he wears a brush instead of feathers for a tail, or that he makes sly visits to the chicken yard after dark? When you see his rusty, reddish-brown coat you guess that the foxy colour of it is alone responsible for his name. His light breast is heavily streaked and spotted with brown, somewhat like a thrush's, and as he is the largest and reddest of the sparrows, it is not at all difficult to identify him.

In the autumn, when the juncos come into the United States from Canada, small flocks of their fox sparrow cousins, that have spent the summer from the St. Lawrence region and Manitoba northward to Alaska, may also be expected. They are often seen in the junco's company among the damp thickets and weeds, along the roadsides and in stalky fields bounded by woodland. The fox sparrow loves to scratch among the dead leaves for insects trying to hide there, quite as well as if he were a chicken or a towhee or an oven-bird who kick up the leaves and earth rubbish after his vigorous manner.

From Virginia southward, the people know the fox sparrow only as a winter resident. Before he leaves them in the spring, he begins to practise the clear, rich, ringing song, which fairly startles one with pleasure the first time it is heard.

JUNCO

Called also: Slate-coloured Snow-bird

When the skies are leaden and the first flurries of snow warn us that winter is near, flocks of juncos, that reflect the leaden skies on their backs, and the grayish-white snow on their breasts, come from the North to spend the winter. A few enter New England as early as September, but by Thanksgiving increased numbers are foraging for their dinner among the roadside thickets, in the furrows of ploughed fields, on the ground near evergreens, about the barn-yard and even at the dog's plate beyond the kitchen door.

Notice how abruptly the slate gray colour of the junco's mantle ends in a straight line across his light breast, and how, when he flies away, the white feathers on either side of his tail serve as signals to his friends to follow. Such signals are especially useful when birds are migrating; without them, many stragglers from the flocks might get lost. Juncos, who are extremely sociable birds, except when nesting, need help in keeping together. A crisp, frosty *'tsip* call note signifies alarm and away flies the flock. They are quiet, unassuming visitors, modest in manner and in dress; but how we should miss them from the winter landscape!

SNOWFLAKE

In the northern United States and Canada, it is the snowflake or snow bunting, a sparrowy little bird with a great deal of white among its rusty brown feathers that is the familiar winter visitor. Instead of hopping, like most of its tribe, it walks over the frozen fields and rarely perches higher than a bush or fence rail, for it comes very near being a ground bird. Delighting in icy blasts and snow storms, flocks of these irrepressibly cheerful little foragers fatten on a seed diet picked up where other birds would starve.

AMERICAN GOLDFINCH

Called also: Black-winged Yellow-bird; Thistle Bird; Lettuce Bird; Wild Canary

Have you a garden gay with marigolds, sunflowers, coreopsis, zinnias, cornflowers, and gaillardias? If so, every goldfinch in your neighbourhood knows it and hastens there to feed on the seeds of these plants as fast as they form, so that you need expect to save none for next spring's planting. Don't you prefer the birds when flower seeds cost only five cents a packet? Clinging to the slender, swaying stems, the goldfinches themselves look so like yellow flowers that you do not suspect how many are feasting in the garden until they are startled into flight. Then away they go, bounding along through the air, now rising, now falling, in long aerial waves peculiar to them alone. You can always tell a goldfinch by its wavy course through the air. Often it accents the rise of each wave as it flies by a ripple of sweet, twittering notes. The yellow warbler is sometimes called a wild canary because he looks like a canary; the goldfinch has the same misleading name applied to him because he sings like one.

But goldfinches by no means depend upon our gardens for their daily fare. Wild lettuce, mullein, dandelion, ragweed and thistles are special favourites. Many weed stalks suddenly blossom forth into black and gold when a flock of finches alight for a feast in the summer fields, or, browned by winter frost, bend beneath the weight of the birds when they cling to them protruding through the snow.

Usually not until July, when the early thistles furnish plenty of fluff for nest lining, do pairs of goldfinches withdraw from flocks to begin the serious business of raising a family. A compact, cozy, cup-like structure of fine grass, vegetable fibre, and moss, is placed in the crotch of a bush or tree, or sometimes in a tall, branching thistle plant. Except the cedar waxwings, the goldfinches are the latest nesters of all our birds. As their love-making is prolonged through the entire summer, so is the deliciously sweet, tender, canary-like song of the male. *Dear, dear, dearie,* you may hear him sing to his dearest all day long.

In summer, throughout his long courtship, he wears a bright, lemon-yellow wedding suit with black cap, wings, and tail, while his sweetheart is dressed in a duller green or olive yellow. After the August moult, he emerges a dingy olive-brown, sparrowy bird, in perfect colour harmony with the wintry fields.

PURPLE FINCH

Called also: Linnet

It would seem as if the people who named most of our birds and wild flowers must have been colour-blind. Old rose is more nearly the colour of this finch who looks like a brown sparrow that had been dipped into a bath of raspberry juice and left out in the sun to fade. But only the mature males wear this colour, which is deepest on their head, rump, and breast. Their sons are decidedly sparrowy until the second year and their wives look so much like the song sparrows that you must notice their heavy, rounded bills and forked tails to make sure they are not their cousins. A purple finch that had been caged two years gradually turned yellow, which none of his kin in the wild state has ever been known to do. Why? No ornithologist is wise enough to tell us, for the colour of birds is still imperfectly understood.

Like the goldfinches, these finches wander about in flocks. You see them in the hemlock and spruce trees feeding on the buds at the tips of the branches, in the orchard pecking at the blossoms on the fruit trees, in the wheat fields with the goldfinches destroying the larvæ of the midge, or by the roadsides cracking the seeds of weeds that are too hard to open for birds less stout of bill. When it is time to nest, these finches prefer evergreen trees to all others, although orchards sometimes attract them.

A sudden outbreak of spirited, warbled song in March opens the purple finch's musical season, which is almost as long as the song sparrow's. Subdued nearly to a humming in October, it is still a delightful reminder of the

finest voice possessed by any bird in the great
sparrow tribe.   But it is when the singer is in
love that the song reaches its highest ecstasy.
Then he springs into the air just as the yellow-
breasted chat, the oven-bird, and woodcock do
when they go a-wooing, and sings excitedly
while mounting fifteen or twenty feet above
his mate until he drops exhausted at her side.

INDIGO BUNTING

Called also: Indigo-bird.

Every child knows the bluebird, possibly the
kingfisher and the blue jay, too, but there is
only one other bird with blue feathers, the little
indigo bunting, who is no larger than your pet
canary, that you are ever likely to meet unless
you live in the Southwest where the blue grosbeak might be your neighbour.   If, by chance,
you should see a little lady indigo-bird you
would probably say contemptuously: "Another
tiresome sparrow," and go on your way, not
noticing the faint glint of blue in her wings and
tail.   Otherwise her puzzling plumage is decidedly sparrowy, although unstreaked.   So is
that of her immature sons.   But her husband
will be instantly recognised because he is the
only very small bird who wears a suit of
deep, rich blue with verdigris-green reflections

about the head—bluer than the summer sky
which pales where his little figure is outlined
against it.

Mounting by erratic, short flights from the
weedy places and bushy tangles he hunts among
to the branches of a convenient tree, singing as
he goes higher and higher, he remains for a time
on a conspicuous perch and rapidly and repeat-
edly sings. When almost every other bird is
moulting and moping, he warbles with the same
fervour and timbre. Possibly because he has the
concert stage almost to himself in August, he
gets the credit of being a better performer than
he really is. Only the pewee and the red-eyed
vireo, whom neither midday nor midsummer
heat can silence, share the stage with him then.

TOWHEE

Called also: Chewink; Ground Robin; Joree

From their hunting-ground in the blackberry
tangle and bushes that border a neighbouring
wood, a family of chewinks sally forth boldly
to my piazza floor to pick up seed from the
canary's cage, hemp, cracked corn, sunflower
seed, split pease, and wheat scattered about for
their especial benefit. One fellow grew bold
enough to peck open a paper bag. It is a daily
happening to see at least one of the family close

to the door; or even on the window-sill.
The song, the English, the chipping, the field,
and the white-throated sparrows—any one or
all of these cousins—usually hop about with
the chewinks most amicably and with no
greater ease of manner; but the larger chewink
hops more energetically and precisely than any
of them, like a mechanical toy.

Heretofore I had thought of this large, vigorous bunting as a rather shy or at least self-
sufficient bird with no desire to be neighbourly.
His readiness to be friends when sure of the
genuiness of the invitation, was a delightful
surprise. From late April until late October
my softly-whistled *towhee* has rarely failed to
bring a response from some pensioner, either in
the woodland thicket or among the rhododen-
drons next the piazza where the seeds have
been scattered by the wind. *Chewink*, or *towhee*
comes the brisk call from wherever the busy
bunting is foraging. The chickadee, whippoor-
will, phoebe and pewee also tell you their
names, but this bird announces himself by two
names, so you need make no mistake.

Because he was hatched in a ground nest and
loves to scratch about on the ground for insects,
making the dead leaves and earth rubbish fly
like any barnyard fowl, the towhee it often
called the ground robin. He is a little smaller
than robin-redbreast. Looked down upon from

above he appears to be almost a black bird, for his upper parts, throat and breast are very dark where his mate is brownish; but underneath both are grayish white with patches of rusty red on their sides, the colour resembling a robin's breast when its red has somewhat faded toward the end of summer. The white feathers on the towhee's short, rounded wings and on the sides of his tail are conspicuous signals, as he flies jerkily to the nearest cover. You could not expect a bird with such small wings to be a graceful flyer.

Rarely does he leave the ground except to sing his love-song. Then, mounting no higher than a bush or low branch, he entrances his sweetheart, if not the human critic, with a song to which Ernest Thompson Seton supplies the well-fitted words: *Chuck-burr, pill-a will-a-will-a.*

RED-BREASTED GROSBEAK

Among birds, as among humans, it is the father who lends his name to the family, however difficult it may be to know the mother and children by it. Who that had not studied the books would recognise Mrs. Scarlet Tanager by her name? or Mrs. Purple Finch? or Mrs. Indigo Bunting? or Mrs. Rose-breasted Grosbeak? The latter lady has not a rose-coloured feather on her. She is a streaked, brown bird, resembling an overgrown sparrow, with a thick, exaggerated finch bill and a conspicuous, white eyebrow. When her husband wears his winter clothes in the tropics, his feathers are said to be similar to hers, so that even his name, then, does not fit. But when he returns to the United States in May he is, in very truth, a rose-breasted grosbeak. His back is as black as a chewink's; underneath he is grayish white, and a patch of lovely, brilliant, rose colour on his breast, with wing linings of the same shade, make him a splendidly handsome fellow. Perhaps before you get a glimpse of the feathers that are his best means of introduction, you may hear a thin *eek* call-note from some tree-top, or better still, listen to the sweet, pure, mellow, joyously warbled song, now loud and clear, now softly tender, that puts him in the first rank of our songsters.

Few birds so conspicuously dressed risk the safety of their nests either by singing or by being seen near it, but this gentle cavalier not only carries food to his brooding mate but actually takes his turn at sitting upon the pale-greenish, blue-speckled eggs. As a lover, husband, and father he is irreproachable.

A friend who reared four orphan grosbeaks says that they left the nest when about eleven

days old. They were very tame, even affectionate toward him, hopping over his shoulders, head,
knees, and hands without the least fear, and
eating from his fingers. When only ten weeks
old the little boy grosbeaks began to warble.
On being released to pick up their own living
in the garden, these pets repaid their foster-
father by eating quantities of potato-bugs,
among other pests. Some people call this
grosbeak the potato-bug bird.

CARDINAL GROSBEAK

*Called also : Crested Redbird: Virginia Night-
ingale.*

It was on a cold January day in Central Park,
New York, that I first met a cardinal and was
warmed by the sight. Then I supposed that he
must have escaped from a cage, for he is uncommon north of Washington. With tail and
crest erect, he was hopping about rather clumsily
on the ground near the bear's cage, and
picking up bits of broken peanuts that had
missed their mark. Presently a dove-coloured
bird, lightly washed with dull red, joined him
and I guessed by her crest that she must be
his mate. Therefore both birds were per-
manent residents in the park and not escaped
pets. Although they look as if they belonged

in the tropics, cardinals never migrate as the
rose-breasted grosbeak and so many of our
fair-weather feathered friends do. That is
because they can live upon the weed seeds and
the buds of trees and bushes in winter as
comfortably as upon insects in summer. It
pays not to be too particular.

In the Southern States every child knows the
common cardinal and could tell you that he is
a little smaller than a robin (not half so graceful),
that he is red all over, except a small black
area around his red bill, and that he wears his
head-feathers crested like the blue jay and the
titmouse. In a Bermuda garden, a shelf restaurant nailed up in a cedar tree attracted cardinals about it every hour of the day. If you
can think of a prettier sight than that dark
evergreen, with the brilliant red birds hopping
about in its branches and the sparkling sapphire
sea dashing over gray coral rocks in the back-
ground, do ask some artist to paint it!

Few lady birds sing—an accomplishment
usually given to their lover's only, to help woo
them. But the female cardinal is a charming
singer with a softer voice than her mate's—
most becoming to one of her sex—and an individual song quite different from his loud,
clear whistle.

SNOWY PLOVER

NORTHERN BOBWHITE

WHITE-BREASTED NUTHATCH

CEDAR WAXWING

CHAPTER IX

THE ILL-ASSORTED BLACKBIRD FAMILY

BOBOLINK

Called also: Reedbird; Ricebird; Ortolan; Maybird

Such a rollicking, jolly singer is the bobolink! On a May morning, when buttercups spangle the fresh grasses in the meadows, he rises from their midst into the air with the merriest frolic of a song you ever heard. Loud, clear, strong, full of queer kinks and twists that could not possibly be written down in our musical scale, the rippling, reckless music seems to keep his wings in motion as well as his throat; for when it suddenly bursts forth, up he shoots into the air like a skylark, and paddles himself along with just the tips of his wings while it is the "mad music" that seemingly propels him:—then he drops with his song into the grass again. Frequently he pours out his hilarious melody while swaying on the slender stems of the grasses, propped by the stiff, pointed feathers of his tail. A score or more of bobolinks rising in some open meadow all day long, are worth travelling miles to hear.

If you were to see the mate of one of these merry minstrels apart from him, you might easily mistake her for another of those tiresome sparrows.   A brown, streaked bird, with some buff and a few white feathers, she shades into the colours of the ground as well as they and covers her loose heap of twigs, leaves and grasses in the hay field so harmoniously that few people ever find it or the clever sitter.

As early as the Fourth of July, bobolinks begin to desert the choir, being the first birds to leave us.   Travelling southward by easy stages, they feed on the wild rice in the marshes until, late in August, enormous flocks reach the cultivated rice fields of South Carolina and Georgia.

On the way, a great transformation has gradually taken place in the male bobolink's dress.   At the North he wore a black, buff and white wedding garment, with the unique distinction of being lighter above than below; but this he has exchanged, feather by feather, for a striped, brown, sparrowy winter suit like his mate's and children's, only with a little more buff about it.

In this inconspicuous dress the reedbirds, or ricebirds, as bobolinks are usually called south of Mason and Dixon's line, descend in hordes upon the rice plantations when the grain is in the milk, and do several millions of dollars' worth of damage to the crop every year, sad, sad to tell.   Of course, the birds are snared, shot, poisoned.   In southern markets half a dozen of them on a skewer may be bought, plucked and ready for the oven, for fifty cents or less. Isn't this a tragic fate to overtake our joyous songsters? Birds that have the misfortune to like anything planted by man, pay a terribly heavy penalty.

Such bobolinks as escape death, leave this country by way of Florida and continue their four thousand mile journey to southern Brazil, where they spend the winter; yet, nothing daunted by the tragedies in the rice fields, they dare return to us by the same route in May. By this time the males have made another complete change of feather to go a-courting. Most birds are content to moult once a year, just after nursery duties have ended; some, it is true, put on a partially new suit in the following spring, retaining only their old wing and tail feathers; but a very few, the bobolink, goldfinch, and scarlet tanager among them, undergo as complete a change as Harlequin.

COWBIRD

This contemptible bird every child should know if for no better reason than to despise it. You will see it alone or in small flocks walking about the pastures after the cattle; or, in the

West, boldly perching upon their backs to feed upon the insect parasites — a pleasant visitor for the cows. So far, so good.

The male is a shining, greenish-black bird, smaller than a robin, with a coffee-brown head and neck. His morals are awful, for he makes violent love to any brownish-gray cowbird he fancies but mates with none. What should be his song is a squeaking *kluck tse-e-e*, squeezed out with difficulty, or a gurgle, like water being poured from a bottle. When he goes a-wooing, he behaves ridiculously, parading with spread wings and tail and acting as if he were violently nauseated in the presence of the lady. Fancy a cousin of the musical bobolink behaving so!

And nothing good can be said for the female cowbird. Shirking as she does every motherly duty, she sneaks about the woods and thickets, slyly watching her chance to lay an egg in the cradle of some other bird, since she never makes a nest of her own. Thus she scatters her prospective family throughout the neighbourhood. The yellow warbler, who is a famous sufferer from her visits, sometimes outwits her, as we have seen; but other warblers, less clever, the vireos, some sparrows, and, more rarely, woodpeckers, flycatchers, orioles, thrushes and wrens, seem to accept the unwelcome gift without a protest. If you were a bird so imposed upon, wouldn't you peck holes in that egg, or roll it out of your nest, or build another cradle rather than hatch a big, greedy interloper that would smother and starve your own babies? Probably every cowbird you see has sacrificed the lives of at least part of a brood of valuable, insectivorous songsters. Without the least spark of gratitude in its cold heart, a young cowbird grafter forsakes its over-kind foster parents as soon as it can pick up its living and remains henceforth among its own kin— of whom only cows could think well.

RED-WINGED BLACKBIRD

Called also: Swamp Blackbird

When you are looking for the first pussy willows in the frozen marshes, or listening to the peeping of young frogs some day in early spring, you will, no doubt, become acquainted with this handsome blackbird, with red and orange epaulettes on his shoulders, who has just returned from the South. "*Ke, kong-ker-ee,*" he flutes from the willows and alders about the reedy meadows where he and his bachelor friends flock together and make them ring "with social cheer and jubilee." A little later, flocks of dingy, brown, streaked birds, travelling northward, pause to rest in the marshes. Wholesale courting takes place shortly after and every red-wing in a black uniform chooses one of the plain, streaked, matter-of-fact birds for his mate. The remainder continue their unmaidenly journey in search of husbands, whom they find waiting in cheerful readiness in almost any marsh. By the first of May all have settled down to home life.

Then how constant are the rich, liquid, sweet *o-ka-lee* notes of the red-wing! Ever in foolish fear for the safety of his nest, he advertises its whereabouts in musical headlines from the top of the nearest tree, or circles around it on fluttering wings above the sedges, or *chucks* at any trespasser near it until one might easily torture him by going straight to its site.

But how short-lived is this excessive devotion to his family! In July, the restless young birds flock with the mothers, but the now indifferent fathers keep apart by themselves. Strange conduct for such fussy, solicitous birds! They congregate in large numbers where the wild rice is ripening and make short excursions to the farmers' fields, where they destroy some grain, it is true, but so little as compared with the quantity of injurious insects and weed seed, that the debt is largely in the red-wings' favour.

RUSTY BLACKBIRD

Called also: Thrush Blackbird

This cousin of the red-wing, whom it resembles in size, flight and notes, is a common migrant in the United States. Nesting is done farther north. In spring, the rusty blackbirds come from the South in pairs, already mated, whereas the red-wings and grackles travel then in flocks. At that time the males are a uniform glossy, bluish-black, and their mates a slate gray, darker above than below; but after the summer moult, when they gather in small companies, both are decidedly rusty. You might mistake them for grackles in the spring, but never for male red-wings then with their bright epaulettes. Notice the rusty blackbird's pale yellow eye.

MEADOWLARK

Called also: Old-field Lark; Meadow Starling

Every farmer's boy knows his father's friend, the meadowlark, the brownish, mottled bird, larger than a robin, with a lovely yellow breast and black crescent on it, that keeps well hidden in the grass of the meadows or grain fields. Of course he knows, too, that it is not really a lark, but a starling. When the shy bird takes wing, note the white feathers on the sides of its tail to be sure it is not the big, brownish flicker, who wears a patch of white feathers on its lower back, conspicuous as it flies. The meadowlark has the impolite habit of turning its back upon one as if it thought its yellow breast too beautiful for human eyes to gaze at. It flaps and sails through the air much like bob-white. But flying is not its specialty. It is, however, a strong-legged, active walker, and rarely rises from the ground unless an intruder gets very near, when away it flies, with a nasal, sputtered alarm note, to alight upon a fence rail or other low perch.

The tender, sweet, plaintive, flute-like whistle, *Spring-o'-the-year*, is a deliberate song usually given from some favourite platform—a stump, a rock, a fence or a mound, to which the bird goes for his musical performance only. He sings on and on delightfully, not always the same song, for he has several in his repertoire, and charms all listeners, although he cares to please none but his mate, that looks just like him.

She keeps well concealed among the grasses where her grassy nest is almost impossible to find, especially if it be partly arched over at the top. No farmer who realises what an enormous number of grasshoppers, not to mention other destructive insects, meadow-larks destroy, is foolish enough to let his mowing-machine pass over their nests if he can but locate them. By the time the hay is ready for cutting in June, the active meadowlark babies are usually running about through grassy run-ways, but eggs of the second brood too frequently, alas! meet a tragic end.

ORCHARD ORIOLE

Fortunately many other birds besides this oriole prefer to live in orchards; otherwise think how many worm-eaten apples there would be! He usually has the kingbird for company, and, strange to say, keeps on friendly terms with that rather exclusive fellow; also the robin, the bluebird, the cedar waxwing and several other feathered neighbours who show a preference for fruit trees when it is time to nest. You may know the orchard oriole's cradle by its excellent weaving. It is not a deep, swinging pouch, like the Baltimore oriole's, but a well-rounded cup, more like a vireo's, formed of grasses of nearly even length and width, cut green and woven with far more skill and precision than a basket made by a boy or a girl is apt to be. Look for it near the end of a limb, ten to twenty feet up. It is by no means easily seen when the green, grassy cup matches the colour of the leaves.

The mother oriole is so harmoniously dressed

in grayish olive green, more yellowish underneath, that you may scarcely notice her as she glides among the trees; but her mate is more conspicuous, however quietly dressed in black and reddish chestnut—even sombrely dressed as compared with his flashy orange and black cousin, the Baltimore oriole. Nevertheless, it takes him two, or possibly three years to attain his fine clothes. By that time his song is rich, sweet and strong.

Do orioles generally take special delight in the music of a piano? An orchard oriole who used to come close to our house to feed on the basket worms dangling from a tamarix bush, returned long after the last worm had been eaten whenever someone touched the keys. And I have known more than one Baltimore oriole to fly about the house, joyously singing, as if attracted and excited by the music in-doors.

BALTIMORE ORIOLE

Called also: Firebird; Golden Robin; Hang-nest; Golden Oriole

A flash of flame among the tender young spring foliage; a rich, high, whistled song from the blossoming cherry trees, and every child knows that the sociable Baltimore oriole has just returned from Central America. Brilliant orange and black feathers like his could no more be concealed than the fiery little redstart's; and as if they alone were not enough to advertise his welcome presence in the neighbourhood, he keeps up a rich, ringing, insistent whistle that you can quickly learn to imitate. You have often started all the roosters in your neighbourhood to crowing, no doubt; even so you can "whistle up" the mystified orioles, who are always disposed to live near our homes. Although the Baltimore oriole has a Southern name, he is really more common at the North, whereas the orchard oriole is more at home south of New England.

Lady Baltimore, who wears a yellowish-olive dress with dusky wings and tail, has the reputation of being one of the finest nest builders in the world. To the end of a branch of some tall shade tree, preferably an elm or willow, although almost any large tree on a lawn or roadside may suit her, she carries grasses, plant fibre, string, or bits of cloth. These she weaves and felts into a perfect bag six or seven inches deep and lines it with finer grasses, hair and wool—a safe, cozy, swinging cradle for her babies.

But, as you may imagine, those babies have a rather hard time when they try to climb out of it into the world. Many a one tumbles to the ground, unable to hold on to the tip of a swaying twig, and not being strong enough to fly. Then what a tremendous fuss the parents make! They cannot carry the youngster up into the tree; they are in deadly fear of cats; they are too worried and excited to leave him alone; but the plucky little fellow usually hops toward the tree and with the help of his sharp claws on the rough bark, flutters his way up to the first limb. People who have brought up broods of orphan orioles say that they are unusually lively, interesting pets. The little girl orioles will attempt, instinctively, to weave worsted, string, grass, or whatever is given them to play with, for of course they never took a lesson in weaving from their expert mother.

THE PURPLE AND THE BRONZED GRACKLES

Called also: Crow Blackbirds

You probably know either one of our two crow blackbirds, similar in size and habits, one with purplish, iridescent plumage, the commonest grackle east of the Alleghanies and south of Massachusetts, and the bronzed grackle, with brassy tints in his black plumage, who overruns the Western country and from Massachusetts northward. Both have uncanny, yellow eyes that make you suspect they may be witches in disguise. Their mates are a trifle smaller and duller.

When the trees are still leafless in earliest spring and the ground is brown and cold, flocks of blackbirds dot the bare trees or take shelter from March winds among their favourite evergreens, or walk solemnly about on the earth like small crows, feeding on fat white grubs and beetles in a business-like way. They are singularly joyless birds. A croaking, wheezy whistle, like the sound of a cart wheel that needs axle-grease, expresses whatever pleasure they may have in life.

Always sociable, living in flocks the entire year through, it is in autumn only that they band together in enormous numbers, and in the West especially, do serious havoc in the cornfields. However, they do incalculable good as insect destroyers, so the farmers must forgive the "maize thieves."

.   .   .   .

Was ever a family so ill-assorted as the blackbird and oriole clan? What traits are common to every member of it? Not one, that I know. Some of the family, as you have seen, are gorgeously clad, like the Baltimore oriole; some quite plainly, like the cowbird; and although black seems to be a prevalent colour in the plumage, the meadowlark, for example, is a brown bird with only a black crescent on its breast. Most of the males are dressed quite differently from their mates, although the female grackles are merely duller. Some of these birds sing exquisitely; others wheeze or croak a few unmusical notes. Some live in huge flocks; some live in couples. Some, like the bobolinks, travel to the tropics and beyond every winter; others, like the meadowlark, can endure the intense cold of the North. Part of the family feed upon the ground, but the oriole branch live in the trees. Devotion to mates and children characterise most of the family, but we cannot overlook the cowbird that neither mates nor takes the slightest care of its offspring. The cowbird builds no nest, while its cousin, the Baltimore oriole, is a famous weaver. The bobolink is a rollicking, jolly fellow; the grackle is solemn, even morose. What a queer family!

CHAPTER X

RASCALS WE MUST ADMIRE

AMERICAN CROW
BLUE JAY
CANADA JAY

AMERICAN CROW

TWO close relatives there are which, like the poor, are always with us—the crow and the blue jay. Both are mischievous rascals, extraordinarily clever, with the most highly developed brains that any of our birds possess. Some men of science believe that, because of their brain power, they rightly belong at the head of the bird class where the thrushes now stand; but who wishes to see a family of songless rogues awarded the highest honours of the class *Aves?*

No bird is so well known to "every child," so admired by artists, so hated by farmers, as the crow, who flaps his leisurely way above the cornfields with a *caw* for friend and foe alike, not caring the least for anyone's opinion of him, good or bad. Perhaps he knows his own true worth better than the average farmer, who has persecuted him with bounty laws, shotgun, and poison for generations. The crow keeps no account of the immense numbers of grubs and larvæ he picks up as he walks after the plough every spring, nor does the farmer, who nevertheless counts the corn stolen as fast as it is planted, and as fast as it ripens, you may be very sure, and puts a price on the robber's head. Yet he knows that corn, dipped in tar before it is put in the ground, will be left alone to sprout. But who is clever enough to keep the crows out of the field in autumn?

How humiliated would humans feel if they realised what these knowing birds must think of us when we set up in our cornfields the absurd-looking scares they so calmly ignore! Some crows I know ate every kernel off every ear around the scare-crow in a neighbour's field, but touched no stalk very far from it, as much as to say: "We take your dare along with your corn, Mr. Silly. If the ox that treadeth out his corn is entitled to his share of it, ought not we, who saved it from grass-hoppers, cutworms, May beetles and other pests, be sharers in the profits?" Granted; but what about eating the farmer's young chickens and turkeys as well as the eggs and babies of little song birds? At times, it must be admitted, the crow's heart is certainly as dark as his feathers; he is as black as he is painted, but happily such cannibalism is apt to be rare. Strange that a bird so tenderly devoted to his own fledglings, should be so heartless to others'!

Toward the end of winter, you may see a pair of crows carrying sticks and trash to the top of some tall tree in the leafless woods, and there, in this bulky cradle, almost as bulky as a squirrel's nest, they raise their family. Young crows may be easily tamed and they make interesting, but very mischievous pets. It is only when crows are nesting that they give up their social, flocking habit.

In winter, if the fields be lean, large picturesque flocks may be seen at dawn streaking across the sky to distant beaches where they feed on worms, refuse and small shellfish. More than one crow has been watched, rising in the air with a clam or a mussel in his claws, dropping it on a rock, then falling after it, as soon as the shell is smashed, to feast upon its contents. The fish crow, a distinct species, never found far inland, although not necessarily seen near water, may be distinguished from our common crow by its hoarser *car*. In some cases it joins its cousins on the beaches. With punctual regularity at sundown, the flocks straggle back inland to go to sleep, sometimes thousands of crows together in a single roost. Many birds have more regular meal hours and bed-time than some children seem to care for. Because crows eat almost anything they can find, and pick up a good living where other birds, more finical or less clever, would starve, they rarely need to migrate; but they are great rovers. There is not a day in the year when you could not find a crow.

BLUE JAY

This vivacious, dashing fellow, harsh-voiced and noisy, cannot be overlooked; for when a brightly coloured bird, about a foot long, roves about your neighbourhood with a troop of screaming relatives, everybody knows it. In summer he keeps quiet, but throws off all restraint in autumn. Hear him hammering at an acorn some frosty morning! How vigorous his motions, how alert and independent! His beautiful military blue, black and white feathers, and crested head, give him distinction.

He is certainly handsome. But is his beauty only skin deep? Does it cover, in reality, a multitude of sins? Shocking stories of murder in the song bird's nest have branded the blue jay with quite as bad a name as the crow's. The brains of fledgings, it has been said, are his favourite tid-bits. But happily scientists, who have turned the searchlight on his deeds, find that his sins have been very greatly exaggerated. Remains of young birds were found in only two out of nearly three hundred blue jays' stomachs analysed. Birds' eggs are more apt to be sucked by both jays and squirrels than are the nestlings to be eaten. Do you ever enjoy an egg for breakfast? Fruit, grain, thin-shelled nuts, and the larger seeds of trees

and shrubs, gathered for the most part in Nature's open store-room, not in man's, are what
the jay chiefly delights in; and these he hides
away, squirrel-fashion, to provide for the rainy
day. More than half of all his food in summer
consists of insects, so you see he is then quite
as useful as his cousin, the crow.

Jays are fearful teasers. How they love
to chase about some poor, blinking, bewildered
owl, in the daylight! *Jay-jay-jay,* you may
hear them scream through the woods. They
mimic the hawk's cry for no better reason,
perhaps, than that they may laugh at the panic
into which timid little birds are thrown at the
terrifying sound. A pet jay I knew could whistle
up the stupid house-dog, who was fooled again
and again. This same jay used to carry all
its beech nuts to a piazza roof, wedge them
between the shingles, and open them there
with ease. An interesting array of hair pins,
matches, buttons, a thimble and a silver spoon
were raked out of his favourite cache under
the eaves.

CANADA JAY

Called also: Whiskey Jack; Moose-bird; Meat-bird

Anyone who has camped in the northern
United States and over the Canadian border
knows that the crow and blue jay have a rogue for

a cousin in this sleek, bold thief, the Canada jay.
He is a fluffy, big, gray bird, without a crest, with
a white throat and forehead and black patch
at the back of his neck. This rascal will walk
alone or with his gang into your tent, steal
your candles, matches, venison, and collar-
buttons before your eyes, or help himself to
the fish bait while he perches on your canoe,
or laugh at you with an impudent *ca-ca-ca* from
the mountain ash tree where he and his friends
are feasting on the berries; then glide to the
ground to slyly pick a trap set for mink or
marten. Fortunate the trapper who, on his
return, does not find either bait gone, or game
damaged.

Fearless, amazingly hardy (having been
hatched in zero weather), mischievous and
clever to a maddening degree, this jay, like
his cousins, compels admiration, although we
know all three to be rogues.

CHAPTER XI

THE FLYCATCHERS

THE FLYCATCHERS

WHEN you see a dusky bird, smaller than a robin, lighter gray underneath than on its sooty-brown back, with a well-rounded, erect head, set on a short, thick neck, you may safely guess it is one of the flycatchers—another strictly American family. If the bird has a white band across the end of its tail it is probably the fearless kingbird. If the feathers on top of its head look as if they had been brushed the wrong way into a pointed crest; moreover, if some chestnut colour shows in its tail when spread, and its pearly gray breast shades into yellow underneath, you are looking at the noisy "wild Irishman" of birddom, the crested flycatcher. Confiding Phœbe wears the plainest of dull clothes with a still darker, dusky crown cap, and a line of white on her outer tail feathers. She and the plaintive wood pewee, who has two indistinct whitish bars across her extra-long wings, are scarcely larger than an English sparrow; while the least flycatcher, who calls himself *Chebec*, is, as you may suppose, the smallest member of the tribe to leave the tropics and spend the summer with us. Male and female members of this family wear similar clothes, fortunately for "every child" who tries to identify them.

You can tell a flycatcher at sight by the way he collects his dinner. Perhaps he will be sitting quietly on the limb of a tree or on a fence as if dreaming, when suddenly off he dashes into the air, clicks his broad bill sharply over a winged insect, flutters an instant, then wheels about and returns to his favourite perch to wait for the next course to fly by. He may describe fifty such loops in mid-air and make as many fatal snap-shots before his hunger is satisfied. A swallow or a swift would keep constantly on the wing; a vireo would hunt leisurely among the foliage; a warbler would restlessly flit about the tree hunting for its dinner among the leaves; but the dignified, dexterous flycatcher, like a hawk, waits patiently on his lookout for a dinner to fly toward him. "All things come to him who waits," he firmly believes.

None of the family is musically gifted, but all make a more or less pleasing noise. Flycatchers are solitary, sedentary birds, never being found in flocks; but when mated, they are devoted home lovers.

We are apt to think of tropical birds as very gaily feathered, but certainly many that come from warmer climes to spend the summer with us are less conspicuous than Quakers.

KINGBIRD

Called also: Bee Martin

In spite of his scientific name, which has branded him the tyrant of tyrants, the kingbird is by no means a bully. See him high in air in hot pursuit of that big, black, villainous crow, who dared try to rob his nest, darting about the rascal's head and pecking at his eyes until he is glad to leave the neighbourhood! There seems to be an eternal feud between them. Even the marauding hawk, that strikes terror to every other feathered breast, will be driven off by the plucky little kingbird. But surely a courageous home defender is no tyrant. A kingbird doesn't like the scolding catbird for a neighbour, or the teasing blue jay, or the meddlesome English sparrow, but he simply gives them a wide berth. He is no Don Quixote ready to fight from mere bravado. *Tyrannus tyrannus* is a libel.

For years he has been called the bee martin and some scientific men in Washington determined to learn if that name, also, is deserved. So they collected over two hundred kingbirds from different parts of the country, examined their stomachs and found bees—mostly drones—in only fourteen. The bird is too keen sighted and clever to snap up knowingly a bee with a sting attached, you may be sure; but occasionally he makes a mistake when, don't you believe, he is more sorry for it than the beekeeper? He destroys so many robber flies—a pest of the hives—that the intelligent apiarist, who keeps bees in his orchard to fertilise the blossoms, always likes to see a pair of kingbirds nesting in one of his fruit trees. The gardener welcomes the bird that eats rose chafers; the farmer approves of him because he catches the gadfly that torments his horses and cattle, as well as the grasshoppers, katydids and crickets that would destroy his field crops if left unchecked.

From a favourite lookout on a tall mullein stalk, a kingbird neighbour of mine would detect an insect over one hundred and seventy feet away, where no human eye could see it, dash off, snap it safely within his bill, flutter uncertainly an instant, then return to his perch ready to "loop the loop" again any moment. The curved clasp at the tip of his bill and the stiff hairs at the base helped hold every insect his prisoner. While waiting for food to fly into sight the watcher did a good deal of calling. His harsh, chattering note, *ching*, *ching*, which penetrated to a surprising distance, did not express alarm, but rather the exultant joy of victory.

He and his mate were certainly frantic with

fear, however, when I climbed into their apple tree one June morning, determined to have a peep at the five creamy-white eggs, speckled with brown and pale lilac, that had just been laid in the nest in a crotch near the end of a stout limb. Whirling and dashing about my head, the pair made me lose my balance, and I tumbled ten feet or more to the ground. As the intruder fell, they might well have exclaimed—perhaps they did—"*Sic semper tyrannis!*"

CRESTED FLYCATCHER

Far more tyrannical than the kingbird is this "wild Irishman," as John Burroughs calls the large flycatcher with the tousled head and harsh, uncanny voice, who prowls around the woods and orchards startling most feathered friends and foes with a loud, piercing exclamation that sounds like *What!* Unlike good children, he is more often heard than seen.

That the solitary, unpopular bird takes a mischievous delight in scaring its enemies, you may know when I tell you that it likes better than any other lining for its nest, a cast snake skin. Is it any wonder that the baby flycatchers' hair stands on end? If the great-crest cannot find the skin of a snake to coil around her eggs, or to hang out of the nest, she may use onion skins, or oiled paper, or even fish scales; for what was once a protective custom, sometimes becomes degraded into a cheap imitation of the imitation in the furnishing of her house. Into an abandoned woodpeckers' hole or a bluebirds' cavity after the babies of these early nesters have flown, or into some unappropriated hollow in a tree, this flycatcher carries enough grasses, weeds and feathers to keep her nestlings cozy during those rare days of June beloved by Lowell, but which Dr. Holmes observed are often so rare they are raw.

PHŒBE

Called also: Bridge Pewee; Dusky Flycatcher; Water Pewee

The first of its family to come North, as well as the last to leave us for the winter, the phœbe appears toward the end of March to snap up the first insects warmed into life by the spring sunshine. Grackles in the evergreens, redwings in the swampy meadows, bluebirds in the orchard may assure us that summer is on the way; but the homely, confiding phœbe, who comes close about our houses and barns, brings the good news home to us every hour.

Pewit—phœbe, pewit—phœbe, he calls continually. As he perches on the peak of a building or other point of vantage, notice how vigorously he wags his tail when he calls, and turns his head this way and that, to keep an eye in all directions lest a bite should fly by him unawares.

Presently a mate comes from somewhere south of the Carolinas where she has passed the winter; for phœbes are more hardy than the rest of the family and do not travel all the way to the tropics. With unfailing accuracy she finds the region where she built her nest the previous season or where she herself was hatched. This instinct of returned direction is marvellous, is it not? Sometimes it is hard enough for us humans to find the way home when not ten miles away. Did you ever get lost? Birds almost never do.

Phœbes like a covering over their heads to protect their nests from spring rains, so you will see a domesticated couple going about the place like a pair of wrens, investigating niches under the piazza roof, beams in an empty barn loft and projections under bridges and trestles. By the middle of April a neat nest of moss and lichen, plastered together with mud and lined with long hair or wool, if sheep are near, is made in the vicinity of their home of the year before. The nursery is exquisitely fashioned—

one of the best pieces of bird architecture you are likely to find.

Some over-thrifty housekeepers, nevertheless, tear down nests from their piazzas, because the poor little phœbes are so afflicted with lice that they are considered objectionable neighbours. Many wild birds, like chickens, have their life-blood drawn by these minute pests. But a thorough dusting of the phœbe's nest with Persian powder would bring relief to the tormented birds, save their babies, perhaps, from death and keep the piazza free from vermin. No birds enjoy a bath in your fountain or water pan more than these tormented ones.

From purely selfish motives it pays to cultivate neighbours ever on the lookout for flies, wasps, May beetles, click beetles, elm destroyers and the moth of the cutworm. The first nest is usually so infested that the phœbes either tear it down in July, and build a new one on its site, or else make the second nest at a little distance from the first. The parents of two broods of from four to six ravenously hungry, insectivorous young, with an instinctive desire to return to their old home year after year, should surely meet no discouragement from thinking farmers' wives.

Shouldn't you think that baby phœbes, reared in nests under railroad bridges, would be fearfully frightened whenever a train thundered overhead?

WOOD PEWEE

When you have been wandering through the summer woods did you ever, like Trowbridge, sit down

> "Beside the brook, irresolute,
> And watch a little bird in suit
> Of sombre olive, soft and brown,
> Perched in the maple branches, mute?
> With greenish gold its vest was fringed,
> Its tiny cap was ebon-tinged,
> With ivory pale its wings were barred,
> And its dark eyes were tender starred.
> 'Dear bird,' I said, 'what is thy name?'
> And thrice the mournful answer came,
> So faint and far, and yet so near—
> 'Pewee! pe-wee! peer!' "

Doubtless this demure, gentle little cousin of the noisy, aggressive, crested flycatcher has no secret sorrow preying at its heart, but the tender pathos of its long-drawn notes would seem to indicate that it is rather melancholy. And it sings (in spite of the books which teach us that the flycatchers are "songless, perching birds") from the time of its arrival from Central America in May until only the tireless indigo bunting and the red-eyed vireo are left in the choir in August.

But how suddenly its melancholy languor

departs the instant an insect flies within sight!
With a cheerful, sudden sally in mid-air, it
snaps up the luscious bite, for it can be quite as
active as any of the family. While not so
ready to be neighbourly as the phœbe, the
pewee condescends to visit our orchards and
shade trees.

When nesting time comes, it looks for a partly
decayed, lichen-covered branch, and on to this
saddles a compact, exquisite cradle of fine
grass, moss and shreds of bark, binding bits of
lichen with spiders' web to the outside until
the sharpest of eyes are needed to tell the
stuccoed nest from the limb it rests on. Only
the tiny hummingbird, who also uses lichen as
a protective and decorative device, conceals
her nest so successfully.

LEAST FLYCATCHER

Called also: Chebec

It is not until he calls out his name, *Chebec!
Chebec!* in clear and business-like tones from
some tree-top that you could indentify this
fluffy flycatcher, scarcely more than five inches
long, whose dusky coat and light vest offer no
helpful markings. Not a single gay feather
relieves his sombre suit. Isn't this a queer,
Quakerly taste for a bird that spends half his life

in the tropics among gorgeously feathered friends? Even the plain vireos, as a family, wear finer clothes than the dusky flycatchers. You may know that the chebec is not one of those deliberate searchers of foliage by his sudden, murderous sallies in mid-air.

Abundant from Pennsylvania to Quebec, the least flycatchers are too inconspicuous to be much noticed. They haunt apple orchards chiefly at nesting time, fortunately for the crop, and at no season secrete themselves in shady woods as pewees do. A little chebec neighbour of mine used to dart through the spray from the hose that played on the lawn late every every afternoon during a drought, and sit on the tennis net to preen his wet feathers; but he nearly put out my eyes in his excitement and anger when I presumed on so much friendliness to peep into his nest.

CHAPTER XII

SOME QUEER RELATIONS

WHIP-POOR-WILL

A QUEER, shadowy bird, that sleeps all
day in the dense wood and flies about
through open country after dark as softly as
an owl, would be difficult for any child to know
were it not for the weird, snappy triplets of
notes that tell his name. Every one knows him
far better by sound than by sight. *Whip-
poor-will* (*chuck*) *whip-poor-will* (*chuck*) *whip-
poor-will* (*chuck*) he calls rapidly for about
two hours, just after sunset or before sunrise
from some low place, fluttering his wings at
each announcement of his name. But you
must be near him to hear the *chuck* at the end
of each vigorous triplet; most listeners don't
know it is there.

You might be very close indeed without
seeing the plump bird, about the size of a robin,
who has flattened himself lengthwise against
a lichen-covered branch until you cannot tell
bird from bark. Or he may be on a rock or an
old, mossy log, where he rests serene in the
knowledge that his mottled, dull dark-brown,
gray, buff, black and white feathers blend
perfectly with his resting place. He must
choose a spot broad enough to support his

whole body, for, like his cousin, the nighthawk, and his more distant relatives, the hummingbird and the swift, his feet are too small and weak for much perching. You never see him standing erect on a twig with his toes clasped around it, but always squatting when at rest.

A narrow white band across his throat makes his depressed head look as if it had been separated from his body—a queer effect that may remind you of the Cheshire Cat in "Alice in Wonderland." The whip-poor-will's three outer tail feathers have white ends which help to distinguish him from the nighthawk. He has a funny little short beak, but his large mouth stretches from ear to ear, and when he flies low above the fields after sunset, this trap is kept open, like the swift's and the swallow's, to catch any night-flying insects—mosquitoes, June bugs, gnats, katydids and little moths—that cross his path. Long, stiffened bristles at the ends of his mouth prevent the escape of a victim past the gaping trap. On the wing the bird is exceedingly swift and graceful. Some children mistake him for a bat or a nighthawk.

Relying upon the protective covering of her soft plumage, the mother whip-poor-will builds no nest, but lays a pair of mottled eggs directly on the ground in the dark woods where a carpet of dead leaves and decayed wood makes con-

cealment perfect. Not even the ovenbird con-
trives that a peep at her eggs shall be so difficult
for us. It is next to impossible to find them.
Unlike the wicked cowbird, who builds no nest
because she has no maternal instinct, the whip-
poor-will, who is a devoted mother, makes none
because none is needed. Once I happened upon
two fuzzy, dark, yellowish-gray, baby whip-poor-
wills (mostly mouths) in a hollow of a decayed,
lichen-covered log, which was their "comfy"
cradle; but the frantic mother, who flopped and
tumbled about on the ground around them,
whining like a puppy, sent me running away
from sheer pity.

In the Southern States a somewhat larger
whip-poor-will, but with the same habits, is
known as chuck-will's-widow.

NIGHTHAWK

Called also: Bull-bat; Night-jar; Mosquito-hawk

Did you ever hear a rushing, whirring, booming sound as though wind were blowing
across the bung-hole of an empty barrel? The
nighthawk, who makes it, is such a high flyer,
that in the dusk of the late afternoon or early
evening, when he delights to sail abroad to get
his dinner, you cannot always see him; but as

he coasts down from the sky—not on a sled, but on his half-closed wings—with tremendous speed, the rush of air through his stiff, long wing feathers makes an uncanny, æolian music that silly, superstitious people have declared is a bad omen. You might think he would dash out his brains in such a headlong dive through the air, but before he hits the earth, a sudden turn saves him and off he goes unharmed, skimming above the ground and catching insects after the whip-poor-will's manner. He lacks the helpful bristles at the ends of his fly-trap. Don't imagine, because of his name, that he flies about only at night. He is not so nocturnal in his habits as the whip-poor-will. Toward the end of summer, especially, he may be seen coursing over the open country at almost any hour of the day. Once in a while, as he hunts, he calls *peent*—a sharp cry that reminds you of the meadowlark's nasal call-note. Presently, mounting upward higher and higher, at the leisurely rate of a boy dragging his sled up hill, he seems to reach the very clouds, when down he coasts again, faster than a boy's flexible flyer. Listen for the booming noise of this coaster! Evidently he enjoys the sport as much as any boy or girl, for he repeats his sky-coasting very often without having to wait for a snow-storm. Indeed, when winter comes, he is enjoying another summer in South

America. Life without insects would be impossible for him.

When he is coursing low above the fields, with quick, erratic, bat-like turns, notice the white spots, almost forming a bar across his wings, for they will help you to distinguish him from the whip-poor-will, who carries his white signals on the outer feathers of his tail. Both of these cousins wear the same colours, only they put them on differently, the whip-poor-will having his chiefly mottled, the nighthawk his chiefly barred. The latter wears a broader white band across his throat. His mate substitutes buff for his white decorations.

Like the mother whip-poor-will, she makes no nest but places her two speckled treasures in some sunny spot, either on the bare ground, on a rock, or even on the flat roof of a house. Since electric lights attract so many insects to the streets of towns and villages, the enterprising nighthawk often forsakes the country to rear her children where they may enjoy the benefits of modern improvements.

Both the nighthawk and the whip-poor-will belong to the goatsucker family. Did you ever hear a more ridiculous name? Eighty-five innocent birds of this tribe, found in most parts of the world, have to bear it because some careless observer may have seen one of their number flying among a herd of goats in Europe to catch

the insects on them, just as cowbirds follow
our cattle; and he imagined the bird was
actually drinking the goat's milk!

CHIMNEY SWIFT

There are some children, and grown-ups, too,
who persist in calling this bird the chimney
swallow, although it is not even remotely
related to the swallow family, and its life history, as well as its anatomy, are quite different
from a swallow's, as you shall see.

Down within some unused chimney, the
modern babies of this soot-coloured, dark,
grayish-brown bird first open their eyes.   Old-
fashioned swifts still nest in hollow trees or
caves, but chimneys are so much more abundant
and convenient, that up-to-date birds prefer
them.   Without stopping in their flight, the
parent swifts snap off with their beaks or feet,
little twigs at the ends of dead branches, and
these they carry, one by one, into a chimney,
gluing them against the side until they have
finished an almost flat, shelf-like, lattice cradle.
Where do they get their glue?   Only during
the nesting season do certain glands in their
mouths flow a brownish fluid that quickly gums
and hardens when exposed to the air.   After
nursery duties have ended, the gland shrinks

from disuse. When the basket cradle has been stuck against a chimney-side, it looks as if it were covered with a thin coat of isinglass. On this lattice from four to six white eggs are laid. A friend, who innocently started a fire in his library one cold, rainy mid-summer evening, was startled and shocked when a nest and eggs suddenly fell on the hearth. He had no idea birds were nesting in his chimney. The rush of their wings he had thought was the wind. Of course the fire melted the glue, when down fell the cradle. Happily there were no "babies and all" to tumble into the flames.

When the baby swifts are old enough to climb out of the lattice, they still cling near it for about a fortnight waiting for their wings to grow strong, before they try to leave the chimney. Apparently they hang themselves up to go to sleep. Shouldn't you think they would fall on the hearth down stairs? Doubtless they would but for their short, thin, stiff-pointed tail feathers which help to prop them up where they cling to the rough bricks and mortar of the chimney lining. Woodpeckers also prop themselves with their tail feathers, but against tree trunks. Not until swifts are a month old do the lazy little fellows climb out of their deep, dark cavern into the boundless sky, which is their true home. No birds are more tireless, rapid flyers than they. Their small feet, weak from disuse, could scarcely hold them on a perch.

One day last July I picked up on the ground a young swift I thought had dropped from exhaustion in its first flight. As swifts had been nesting in one of the chimneys, I carried the young bird in my hand into the house, up stairs, out through an attic window onto the roof, climbed along the ridgepole in terror for my life, clinging by only one free hand to the peak of the roof, and at last reached the swift's chimney. Laying the sooty youngster on the stone chimney-cap I had crawled cautiously backward only a few feet, when lo! my charge suddenly bounded off into the air like a veteran to join a flock of companions playing cross-tag. As it wheeled and darted above the house, evidently quite as much at ease in the air as any of the merry, twittering company, don't you believe it started the laugh on me? But what had brought so able a young flyer to earth? My wounded vanity tempts me to believe that it had really dropped from fatigue and, once on the ground, was unable to rise again, whereas it was comparatively easy to launch itself from the chimney-top.

With mouths agape from ear to ear, the swifts draw in an insect dinner piecemeal, as they course through the air, just as the whip-poor-will, nighthawk and swallows do. Fortunate the house where a colony elect to live, for they rid the air of myriads of gnats and mosquitoes, as they fly about overhead, silhouetted against the sky. Early in the morning and late in the afternoon are their hours for exercise. You will think, perhaps, that they look more like bats than birds. Watch their rapid wing-beats very closely and see if you can settle the mooted question as to whether they use both wings at once, or first one wing and then the other in alternate strokes. After you have noticed their peculiar, throbbing flight, you will never again confuse them with the graceful, gliding swallows. Although the swift is actually shorter than a sparrow, its spread wings measure over a foot across from tip to tip. No wonder it can fly every waking moment without feeling tired, and journey from Labrador to Central America for a winter holiday.

RUBY-THROATED HUMMINGBIRD

What child does not know the hummingbird, the jewelled midget that flashes through the garden, poises before a flower as if suspended in the air by magic, thrusts a needle-like bill into one cup of nectar after another, then whirs off out of sight in a trice? It is the smallest bird we have. Suppose a fairy wished to pluck one for her dinner, as we should pluck a chicken; how large, do you think, would be the actual body of a hummingbird, without its feathers? Not much, if any, larger than a big bumble-bee, I venture to guess. Yet this atom of animation travels from Panama to Quebec or beyond, and back again every year of its brief life, that it may live where flowers, and the minute insects that infest them, will furnish drink and meat the year around. So small a speck of a traveller cannot be seen in the sky by an enemy with the sharpest of eyes. Space quickly swallows it. A second after it has left your garden it will be out of sight. This mite of a migrant has plenty of stay-at-home relatives in the tropics—exquisite creatures they are—but the ruby-throat is the only hummingbird bold enough to venture into the eastern United States and Canada.

What tempts him so far north? You know that certain flowers depend upon certain insect friends to carry their pollen from blossom to blossom that they may set fertile seed; but did you know that certain other flowers depend upon the hummingbird ? Only his tongue, that may be run out beyond his long, slender bill and turned around curves, could reach the drops of nectar in the tips of the wild columbine's five inverted horns of plenty. The

Monarda or bee-balm, too, hides a sweet sip in each of its red tubes for his special benefit. So does the coral honeysuckle. There are a few other flowers that cater to him, especially, by wearing his favourite colour, by hiding nectar so deep that only his long tongue can drain it, and by opening in orderly succession so that he shall fare well throughout the summer, not have a feast one month and a famine the next. In addition to these flowers in Nature's garden that minister to his needs, many that have been brought from the ends of the earth to our garden plots please him no less. The canna, nasturtium, phlox, trumpet-flower, salvia, and a host of others, delight his eye and his palate. Don't you think it is worth while to plant his favourites in your garden if only for the joy of seeing him about? He is wonderfully neighbourly, coming to the flower-beds or window-boxes with undaunted familiarity in the presence of the family. A hummingbird that lived in my garden sipped from a sprig of honeysuckle that I held in my hand. But the bird is not always so amiable by any means. A fierce duellist, he will lunge his rapier-like bill at another hummer with deadly thrusts. A battle of the midgets in mid-air is a sorry sight.

You may know a male by the brilliant metallic-red feathers on his throat. His mate lacks these, but her brilliancy has another outlet, for she is one of the most expert nest-builders in the world. An exquisitely dainty little cup of plant down, felted into a compact cradle and stuccoed with bits of lichen bound on by spider-web, can scarcely be told from a knot on the limb to which it is fastened. Two eggs, not larger than beans, in time give place to two downy hummers about the size of honey-bees. Perhaps you have seen pigeons pump food down the throats of their squabs? In this same way are baby hummingbirds fed. After about three weeks in the nest, the young are ready to fly; but they rest on perches the first month of their independence more than at any time afterward. No weak-footed relative of the swift could live long off the wing. It is good-bye to summer when the last hummingbird forsakes our frost-nipped, northern gardens for happier hunting grounds far away.

CHAPTER XIII

NON-UNION CARPENTERS

OUR FIVE COMMON WOODPECKERS

IF, AS you walk through some old orchard or along the borders of a woodland tangle, you see a high-shouldered, stocky bird clinging fast to the side of a tree "as if he had been thrown at it and stuck," you may be very sure he is a woodpecker. Four of our five common, non-union carpenters wear striking black and white suits, patched or striped, the males with red on their heads, their wives with less of this jaunty touch of colour perhaps, or none, but wearing otherwise similar clothes. Only the dainty little black and white creeping warbler could possibly be confused with the smallest of these sturdy, matter-of-fact artisans, although, as you know, chickadees, titmice, nuthatches and kinglets also haunt the bark of trees; but the largest of these is smaller than downy, the smallest of the woodpeckers. One of the carpenters, the big flicker, an original fellow, is dressed in soft browns, yellow, white and black, with the characteristic red patch across the back of his neck.

It is easy to tell a woodpecker at sight or even beyond it, when you see or hear him hammering for a dinner, or drumming a love song, or chiselling out a home in some partly decayed tree. How cheerfully his vigorous taps resound! Hammer, chisel, pick, drill, and drum—all these instruments in one stout bill—and a flexible barbed spear for a tongue that may be run out far beyond his bill, like the hummingbird's, make the woodpecker the best-equipped workman in the woods. All the other birds that pick insect eggs, grubs, beetles and spiders from the bark could go all over a tree and feast, but the woodpecker might follow them and still find plenty left, borers especially, hidden so deep that only his sticky, barbed tongue could drag them out.

As you see his body flattened against the tree's side perhaps you wonder why he doesn't fall off. Do you remember why the swifts, that sleep against the inside walls of our chimneys, do not fall down to the hearths below? Like them and the bobolink, the woodpeckers prop themselves by their outspread, stiffened tails. Moreover, they have their toes arranged in a curious way—two in front and two behind, so that they can hold on to a section of bark very much as an iceman holds a piece of ice between his tongs. Smooth bark conceals no larvæ nor does it offer a foothold, which is why you are likely to see woodpeckers only on the trunks or the larger limbs of trees where old, scaly bark grows.

DOWNY WOODPECKER

A hardy little friend is the downy wood-pecker who, like the chickadee, stays by us the year around. Probably no other two birds are so useful in our orchards as these, that keep up a tireless search for the insect robbers of our fruit. Wintry weather can be scarcely too severe for either, for both wear a warm coat of fat under their skins and both have the comfort of a snug retreat when bitter blasts blow.

Friend downy is too good a carpenter, you may be sure, to neglect making a cozy cavity for himself in autumn, just as the hairy wood-pecker does. The chickadee, titmouse, nut-hatch, bluebird, wren, tree swallow, sparrow hawk, crested flycatcher and owls, are not the only birds that are thankful to occupy his snug quarters in some old tree after he has moved out in the spring to the new nursery that his mate and he make for their family. He knows the advantage of a southern exposure for his hollow home and chisels his winter quarters deep enough to escape a draught. Here he lives in single blessedness—or selfishness?—with no thought now for the comfort of his mate, who, happily, is quite as good a carpenter as he, and as able to care for herself. She may make a winter home or keep the nursery.

Very early in the spring you will hear the downy, like the other woodpeckers, beating a rolling tattoo on some resonant limb, and if you can creep close enough you will see his head hammering so fast that there is only a blur above his shoulders. This drumming is his love song. The grouse is even a more wonderful performer, for he drums without a drum, which no woodpecker can do. The woodpecker drums not only to win a mate, however, but to tell where a tree is decayed and likely to be an easy spot to chisel, and also to startle borers beneath the bark, that he may know just where to tunnel for them, when they move with a faint noise, which his sharp ears instantly detect.

This master workman, who is scarcely larger than an English sparrow, occasionally pauses in his hammering long enough to utter a short, sharp *peek*, *peek*, often continued into a rattling cry that ends as abruptly as it began. You may know him from his larger and louder-voiced cousin, the hairy woodpecker, not only by this call note, but by the markings of the outer tail feathers, which, in the downy, are white barred with black; and in the hairy, are white without the black bars. Both birds are much striped and barred with black and white.

When the weather grows cold, hang a bone with a little meat on it, cooked or raw, or a lump of suet in some tree beyond the reach of cats; then watch for the downy woodpecker's and the chickadee's visits to your free-lunch counter.

HAIRY WOODPECKER

Light woods, with plenty of old trees in them, suit this busy carpenter better than orchards or trees close to our homes, for he is more shy than his sociable little cousin, downy, whom he as closely resembles in feathers as in habits. He is three inches longer, however, yet smaller than a robin. In spite of his name, he is covered with black and white feathers, not hairs. He has a hairy stripe only down the middle of his broadly striped back.

After he and his mate have decided to go to housekeeping, they select a tree—a hollow-hearted or partly decayed one is preferred—and begin the hard work of cutting out a deep cavity. Try to draw freehand a circle by making a series of dots, as the woodpecker outlines his round front door, and see, if you please, whether you can make so perfect a ring. Downy's entrance need be only an inch and a half across; the hairy's must be a little larger, and the flicker requires a hole about four inches in diameter to admit his big body. Both mates work in turn at the nest hole. How the chips fly! Braced in position by stiff tail feathers and clinging by his stout toes, the woodpecker keeps hammering and chiselling at his home more hours every day than a labour union would allow. Two inches of digging with his strong combination tool means a hard day's work. The hole usually runs straight in for a few inches, then curves downward into a pear-shaped chamber large enough for a comfortable nursery. A week or ten days may be spent by a couple in making it. The chips by which this good workman is known are left on the nursery floor, for woodpeckers do not pamper their babies with fine grasses, feathers or fur cradle linings, as the chickadee and some other birds do. A well-regulated woodpecker's nest contains five glossy-white eggs.

Sheltered from the rain, wind and sun, hidden from almost every enemy except the red squirrel, woodpecker babies lie secure in their dark, warm nursery, with no excitement except the visits of their parents with a fat grub. Then how quickly they scramble up the walls toward the light and dinner!

YELLOW-BELLIED SAPSUCKER

This woodpecker I am sorry to introduce to you as the black sheep of his family, with scarcely a friend to speak a good word for him.

Murder is committed on his immensely useful relatives, who have the misfortune to look ever so little like him, simply because ignorant people's minds are firmly fixed in the belief that every woodpecker is a sapsucker, therefore a tree-killer, which only this miscreant is, and very rarely. The rest of the family who drill holes in a tree harmlessly, even beneficially, do so because they are probing for insects. The sapsucker alone drills rings or belts of holes for the sake of getting at the soft inner bark and drinking the sap that trickles from it.

Mrs. Eckstorm, who has made a careful study of the woodpeckers in a charming little book that every child should read, tells of a certain sapsucker that came silently and early in the autumn mornings to feed on a favourite mountain ash tree near her dining-room window. In time this rascal killed the tree. "Early in the day he showed considerable activity," writes Mrs. Eckstorm, "flitting from limb to limb and sinking a few holes, three or four in a row, usually *above* the previous upper girdle of the limbs he selected to work upon. After he had tapped several limbs, he would sit patiently waiting for the sap to flow, lapping it up quickly when the drop was large enough. At first he would be nervous, taking alarm at noises and wheeling away on his broad wings till his fright was over, when he would steal quietly back to his sapholes. When not alarmed, his only movement was from one row of holes to another, and he tended them with considerable regularity. As the day wore on he became less excitable, and clung cloddishly to his tree trunk with ever increasing torpidity, until finally he hung motionless as if intoxicated, tippling in sap, a dishevelled, smutty, silent bird, stupefied with drink, with none of that brilliancy of plumage and light-hearted gaiety which made him the noisiest and most conspicuous bird of our April woods."

But it must be admitted that very rarely does the sapsucker girdle a tree with holes enough to sap away its life. He may have an orgie of intemperance once in awhile, but much should be forgiven a bird as dexterous as a flycatcher in taking insects on the wing and with a hearty appetite for pests. Wild fruit and soft-shelled nuts he likes too. He never bores a tree to get insects as his cousins do, for only when a nest must be chiselled out is he a wood *pecker* in the strict sense.

You may know this erring one by the pale, sulphur-yellow tinge on his white under parts, the white patch above the tail on his mottled black and white back, his spotted wings with conspicuous white coverts, the broad black patch on his breast extending to the corners of his mouth in a chin strap, and the lines of crimson on forehead, crown, chin and throat. He is smaller than a robin by two inches, yet larger than the English sparrow, who shares with him a vast amount of public condemnation.

RED-HEADED WOODPECKER

A pair of red-headed woodpeckers I know, who made their home in an old tree next the station yard at Atlanta, where locomotives clanged, puffed, whistled and shrieked all day long, evidently enjoyed the noise, for the male liked nothing better than to add to it by tapping on one of the glass non-conductors around which a telegraph wire ran. When first I saw the handsome, tri-coloured fellow he was almost enveloped in a cloud of smoke escaping from a puffing locomotive on the track next the telegraph pole, yet he tapped away unconcerned and as merrily as you would play a two-step on the piano. When the vapour blew away, his glossy bluish black and white feathers, laid on in big patches, were almost as conspicuous as his red head, throat and upper breast. His mate is red-headed, too.

All the woodpeckers have musical tastes. A flicker comes to my verandah to tap a galvanised rain gutter, for no other reason than the excellent one that he enjoys the sound. Tin roofs everywhere are popular tapping places. Certain dry, dead, seasoned limbs of hardwood trees resound better than others and a woodpecker in love is sure to find out the best one in the spring when he beats a rolling tattoo in the hope of charming his best beloved.   He has no need to sing, which is why he doesn't.

Fence posts are the red-head's favourite resting places.   From these he will make sudden sallies in mid-air, like a fly-catcher, after a passing insect; then return to his post.

You remember that the blue jay has the thrifty habit of storing nuts for the proverbial rainy day, and that the shrike hangs up his meat to cure on a thorn tree like a butcher. Red-headed woodpeckers, who are especially fond of beechnuts, acorns and grasshoppers, hide them away, squirrel fashion, in tree cavities, in fence holes, crevices in old barns, between shingles on the roof, behind bulging boards, in the ends of railroad ties, in all sorts of queer places, to feast upon them in winter when the land is lean.   Who knows whether other woodpeckers have hoarding places?   The sapsucker, the hairy and the downy woodpeckers also like beechnuts; the flicker prefers acorns; but do they store them for winter use? The red-head's thrifty habit was only recently discovered: has it been only recently acquired? It must be simpler to store the summer's surplus than to travel to a land of plenty when winter comes. Heretofore this red-headed cousin has been reckoned a migratory member of the home-loving woodpecker clan, but only where he could not find plenty of beechnuts to keep him through the winter.

FLICKER

Called also: High-hole; Clape; Golden-winged Woodpecker; Yellow-hammer; Yucker

Why should the flicker discard family traditions and wear clothes so different from those of his relations? His upper parts are dusty brown, narrowly barred with black, and the large white patch on his lower back, so conspicuous as he flies from you, is one of the best marks of identification on his big handsome body. His head is gray with a black streak below the eye, and a scarlet band across the nape of the neck, while the upper side of the wing feathers is black relieved by golden shafts. Underneath, the wings are a lovely golden yellow, seen only when the bird flies toward you. His breast, which is a pale, pinkish brown, is divided from the throat by a black crescent, smaller than the meadowlark's, and below this half-moon of jet there are many black spots,

He is quite a little larger than a robin, the largest and the commonest of our five non-union carpenters.

See him feeding on the ground instead of on the striped and mottled tree trunks, where his black and white striped relatives are usually found, and you will realise that he wears brown clothes, finely barred, because they harmonise so perfectly with the brown earth. What does he find on the ground that keeps him there so much of the time? Look at the spot he has just flown from and you will doubtless find ants. These are chiefly his diet. Three thousand of them, for a single meal, he has been known to lick out of a hill with his long, round, extensile, sticky tongue. Evidently this lusty fellow needs no tonic. His tail, which is less rounded than his cousins', proves that he has little need to prop himself against tree trunks to pick out a dinner; and his curved bill, which is more of a pickaxe than a hammer, drill, or chisel, is little used as a carpenter's tool except when a nest is to be dug out of soft, decayed wood. Although he can beat a rolling tattoo in the spring, he has a variety of call notes for use the year through. Did you ever see the funny fellow spread his tail and dance when he goes courting? Flickers condescend to use old holes deserted by their relatives who possess better tools. You must have noticed all through these bird biographies that the structure and colouring of every bird are adapted to its kind of life, each member of the same family varying according to its habits. The kind of food a bird eats and its method of getting it, of course, bring about most, if not all, of the variations from the family type. Each is fitted for its own life, "even as you and I."

Like your pet pigeon, the hummingbird, and several other birds, parent flickers pump partly digested food from their own stomachs into those of their hungry babies. Imagine how many trips would have to be taken to a nest if ants were carried there one by one! How can the birds be sure they will not thrust their bills through the eyes of their blind, naked and helpless babies in so dark a hole? It must be very difficult to find the mouths and be sure none is neglected. Like the little pig you all know about, I suspect there is always at least one little flicker in the dark tree-hollow that "gets none" each trip.

CHAPTER XIV

CUCKOO AND KINGFISHER

YELLOW-BILLED CUCKOO
BLACK-BILLED CUCKOO
BELTED KINGFISHER

YELLOW-BILLED CUCKOO

Called also: Rain Crow

DO YOU own a cuckoo clock with a little bird inside that flies out of a door every hour and tells you the time? Except when it is time to go to school or to bed you are doubtless amused to hear him hiccough *cuckoo, cuckoo,* the mechanical notes that tell his name. Cuckoo clocks were first made in Europe where the common species of cuckoo calls in this way, but don't imagine its American cousins do. Our yellow-billed cuckoo's unmusical, guttural notes sound something like a tree toad's rattle, *kuk-kuk, kuk-kuk, kuk-kuk, kr-r-r-uck, kr-r-r-uck, kr-r-r-uck, kr-r-ruck, cow, cow, cow, cow!* This is his complete "song," but usually one hears only a portion of it. The black-billed cuckoo's voice is softer, and its *cow* notes run together, otherwise their "songs" are alike.

Both of our common cuckoos are slim, graceful birds about twelve inches long—longer than a robin. They are solitary creatures and glide silently among the foliage of trees and shrubbery, rarely giving you a good look at their satiny, grayish-brown backs and dull-white breasts. You may know the yellow-billed cuckoo by the yellow lower-half of his long, curved bill, his cinnamon-brown wings and the conspicuous white thumb-nail spots on his dark tail feathers. If you were to dip your thumb in white paint, then pinch these outer quills, you would leave similar marks.

Most birds will not touch the hairy, fuzzy caterpillars—very disagreeable mouthfuls, one would think. But happily cuckoos enjoy them as well as the smooth, slippery kind. "I guess they like the custard inside," said a little boy I know who had stepped on a fat caterpillar on the path. "Cuckoos might well be called caterpillar birds," wrote Florence Merriam Bailey, "for they are so given to a diet of the hairy caterpillars that the walls of their stomachs are actually permeated with the hairs, and a section of stomach looks like the smoothly brushed top of a gentleman's beaver hat." When you see the webs that the tent caterpillar stretches across the ends of the branches of fruit and nut trees toward the end of summer, or early autumn, watch for the cuckoo's visits. Orioles, also, tear open the webs to get at the wiggling morsels inside, but they leave dead and mutilated remains behind them, showing that their appetite for web worms is less keen than that of the cuckoos, who eat them up clean. Fortunately the caterpillar of the terribly destructive gypsy moth is another favourite dainty.

Perhaps you have heard that the cuckoo, like the naughty cowbird, builds no nest and lays its eggs in other birds' cradles? This is true only of the European cuckoo. Its American cousin makes a poor apology for a nest, it is true, merely a loose bundle or platform of sticks, as flimsily put together as a dove's nest. The greenish-blue eggs or the naked babies must certainly fall through, one would think. Still it is all the cuckoos' own, and they are proud of it. But so sensitive and fearful are they when a human visitor inspects their nursery that they will usually desert it, never to return, if you touch it, so beware of peeping!

When the skinny cuckoo babies are a few days old, blue pin-feathers begin to appear, and presently their bodies are stuck full of fine, sharply pointed quills like a well-stocked pin cushion. Porcupine babies you might think them now. But presto! every pin-feather suddenly fluffs out the day before the youngsters leave the nest, and they are clothed in a suit of soft feathers like their parents. In a few months young cuckoos, hatched as far north as New England and Canada or even Labrador, are strong enough to fly to Central or South America to spend the winter.

BELTED KINGFISHER

Called also: The Halcyon

This Izaak Walton of birddom, whom you
may see perched as erect as a fish hawk on a
snag in the lake, creek or river, or on a dead
limb projecting over the water, on the lookout
for minnows, chub, red fins, samlets or any
other small fry that swims past, is as expert as
any fisherman you are ever likely to know.
Sharp eyes are necessary to see a little fish
where sunbeams dance on the ripples and the
refracted light plays queer tricks with one's
vision.   Once a victim is sighted, how swiftly
the lone fisherman dives through the air and
water after it, and how accurately he strikes
its death-blow behind the gills! If the fish be
large and lusty it may be necessary to carry it
to the snag and give it a few sharp knocks with
his long powerful bill to end its struggles.
These are soon over, but the kingfisher's have
only begun.   See him gag and writhe as he
swallows his dinner, head first, and then, re-
gretting his haste, brings it up again to try a
wider avenue down his throat! Somebody
shot a kingfisher which had tried to swallow so
large a fish that the tail was sticking out of his
mouth, while its head was safely stored below
in the bird's stomach.   After the meat digests,

the indigestible skin, bones, and scales of the fish are thrown up without the least nausea.

A certain part of a favourite lake or stream this fisherman patrols with a sense of ownership and rarely leaves it. Alone, but self-satisfied, he clatters up and down his beat as a policeman, going his rounds, might sound his rattle from time to time. The rattle-headed bird knows every pool where minnows play, every projection along the bank where a fish might hide, and is ever on the alert, not only to catch a dinner, but to escape from the sight of the child who intrudes on his domain and wants to "know" him. You cannot mistake this big, chunky bird, fully a foot long, with grayish-blue upper parts, the long, strong wings and short, square tail dotted in broken bars of white, and with a heavy, bluish band across his white breast. His mate and children wear rusty bands instead of blue. The crested feathers on top of his big, powerful head reach backward to the nape like an Indian chief's feather bonnet, and give him distinction. Under his thick, oily plumage, as waterproof as a duck's, he wears a suit of down underclothing.

No doubt you have heard that all birds are descended from reptile ancestors; that feathers are but modified scales, and that a bird's song is but the glorified hiss of the serpent. Then the kingfisher and the bank swallow retain at least one ancient custom of their ancestors, for they still place their eggs in the ground. The lone fisherman chooses a mate early in the spring and, with her help, he tunnels a hole in a bank next a good fishing ground. A minnow pool furnishes the most-approved baby food. Perhaps the mates will work two or three weeks before they have tunnelled far enough to suit them and made a spacious nursery at the end of the long hall. Usually from five to eight white eggs are laid about six feet from the entrance on a bundle of grass, or perhaps on a heap of ejected fish bones and refuse. While his queen broods, the devoted kingfisher brings her the best of his catch. At first their babies are as bare and skinny as their cuckoo relatives. When the father or mother bird flies up stream with a fish for them, giving a rattling call instead of ringing a dinner bell, all the hungry youngsters rush forward to the mouth of the tunnel; but only one can be satisfied each trip. Then all run backward through the inclined tunnel, like reversible steam engines, and keep tightly huddled together until the next exciting rattle is heard. Both parents are always on guard to drive off mink, rats and water snakes that are the terrors of their nursery.

CHAPTER XV

DAY AND NIGHT ALLIES OF THE FARMER

TURKEY VULTURE
RED-SHOULDERED HAWK
RED-TAILED HAWK
COOPER'S HAWK
BALD EAGLE
AMERICAN SPARROW HAWK
AMERICAN OSPREY
AMERICAN BARN OWL
SHORT-EARED OWL
LONG-EARED OWL
BARRED OWL
SCREECH OWL

TURKEY VULTURE

Called also: Turkey Buzzard

EVERY child south of Mason and Dixon's line knows this big buzzard that sails serenely with its companions in great circles, floating high overhead, now rising, now falling, with scarcely a movement of its wide-spread wings. In the air, it expresses the very poetry of motion. No other bird is more graceful and buoyant. One could spend hours watching its fascinating flight. But surely its earthly habits express the very prose of existence; for it may be seen in the company of other dusky scavengers, walking about in the roads of the smaller towns and villages, picking up refuse; or, in the fields, feeding on some dead animal. Relying upon its good offices, the careless farmer lets his dead pig or horse or chicken lie where it dropped, knowing that buzzards will speedily settle on it and pick its bones clean. Our soldiers in the war with Spain say that the final touch of horror on the Cuban battlefields was when the buzzards, that were wheeling overhead, suddenly dropped where their wounded or dead comrades fell.

Because it is so helpful in ridding the earth of decaying matter, the law and the Southern people, white and coloured, protect the vulture. Its usefulness is more easily seen and understood than that of many smaller birds of greater value which, alas! are a target for every gunner. Consequently, it is perhaps the commonest bird in the South, and tame enough for the merest tyro in bird lore to learn that it is about two and a half feet long, with a wing spread of fully six feet; that its head and neck are bare and red like a turkey's, and that its body is covered with dusky feathers edged with brown—an ungainly, unlovely creature out of its element, the air. Another sable scavenger, the black vulture or carrion crow, of similar habits, but with a more southerly range, is common in the Gulf States.

Because it feeds on carrion that not even a goat grudges it, and is too lazy and cowardly to pick a quarrel, the buzzard has no enemies. Although classed among birds of prey, it does not frighten the smallest chick in the poultry yard when it flops down beside it. With beak and claws capable of gashing painful wounds, it never uses them for defence, but resorts to the disgusting trick of throwing up the contents of its stomach over any creature that comes too near. When a colony of the ever-sociable buzzards are nesting, you may be very sure no one cares to make a close study of their young.

RED-SHOULDERED HAWK

Called also: Hen Hawk; Chicken Hawk; Winter Hawk

Let any one say "Hawk" to the average farmer and he looks for his gun. For many years it was supposed that every member of the hawk family was a villain and fair game, but the white searchlight of science shows us that most of the tribe are the farmers' allies, which, with the owls, share the task of keeping in check the mice, moles, gophers, snakes, and the larger insect pests. Nature keeps her vast domain patrolled by these vigilant watchers by day and by night. Guns may well be turned on those blood-thirsty fiends in feathers, Cooper's hawk, the sharp-shinned hawk, and the goshawk, that not only eat our poultry, but every song bird they can catch: the law of the survival of the fittest might well be enforced with lead in their case. But do let us protect our friends, the more heavily built and slow-flying hawks with the red tails and red shoulders, among other allies in our ceaseless war against farm vermin!

In the court of last appeal to which all our

hawks are brought—I mean those scientific men in the Department of Agriculture, Washington, who examine the contents of birds' stomachs to learn just what food is taken in different parts of the country and at different seasons of the year—the two so-called "hen hawks" were proved to be rare offenders, and great helpers. Two hundred and twenty stomachs of red-shouldered hawks were examined by Dr. Fisher, and only three contained remains of poultry, while one hundred and two contained mice; ninety-two, insects; forty, moles and other small mammals; fifty-nine, frogs and snakes, and so on. The percentage of poultry eaten is so small that it might be reduced to nothing if the farmers would keep their chickens in yards instead of letting them roam to pick up a living in the fields, where the temptation to snatch up one must be overwhelming to a hungry hawk. Fortunately these two benefi- cent "hen hawks," are still common, in spite of our ignorant persecution of them for two hundred years or more.

Toward the end of summer, especially in September, when nursery duties have ended for the year and the hawks are care free, you may see them sailing in wide spirals, delighting in the cooler stratum of air high overhead. Balancing on wide, outstretched wings, floating serenely with no apparent effort, they enjoy the slow merry-go-round at a height that would make any child dizzy. Sometimes they rise out of sight. *Kee you, kee you,* they scream as they sail. Does the teasing blue jay imitate the call for the fun of frightening little birds?

But the red-shouldered hawk is not on pleasure bent much of the time. Perching is its specialty, and on an outstretched limb, or other point of vantage, it sits erect and dignified, its far-seeing eyes alone in motion trying to sight its quarry—a mouse creeping through the meadow, a mole leaving its tunnel, a chipmunk running along a stone wall, a frog leaping into the swamp, a gopher or young rabbit frisking around the edges of the wood—when, spying one, "like a thunderbolt it falls."

If you could ever creep close enough to a red-shouldered hawk, which is not likely, you would see that it is a powerful bird, about a foot and a half long, dark brown above, the feathers edged with rusty, with bright chestnut patches on the shoulders. The wings and dark tail are barred with white, so are the rusty-buff under parts, and the light throat has dark streaks. Female hawks are larger than the males, just as the squaws in some Indian tribes are larger than the braves. It is said that hawks remain mated for life; so do eagles and owls, for in their family life, at least, the birds of prey are remarkably devoted, gentle and loving.

RED-TAILED HAWK

Called also: Hen Hawk; Chicken Hawk; Red Hawk

This larger relative of the red-shouldered hawk (the female red-tail measures nearly two feet in length) shares with it the hatred of all but the most enlightened farmers. Before condemning either of these useful allies, everyone should read the report of Dr. Fisher, published by the Government, and to be had for the asking. This expert judge tells of a pair of red-tailed hawks that reared their young for two successive seasons in a birch tree in some swampy woods, about fifty rods from a poultry farm, where they might have helped themselves to eight hundred chickens and half as many ducks; yet they were never known to touch one. Occasionally, in winter especially, when other food is scarce, a red-tail will steal a chicken—probably a maimed or sickly one that cannot get out of the way—or drop on a bob-white; but ninety per cent. of its food consists of injurious mammals and insects.

Both of these slandered "hen hawks" prefer to live in low, wet, wooded places with open meadows for hunting grounds near by.

COOPER'S HAWK

Called also: Chicken Hawk; Big Blue Darter

Here is no ally of the farmer, but his foe, the most bold of all his robbers, a blood-thirsty villain that lives by plundering poultry yards, and tearing the warm flesh from the breasts of game and song birds, one of the few members of his generally useful tribe that deserves the punishment ignorantly meted out to his innocent relatives. Unhappily, it is perhaps the most common hawk in the greater part of the United States, and therefore does more harm than all the others. It is mentioned in this chapter that concerns the farmers' allies, only because every child should know foe from friend.

The female Cooper's hawk is about nineteen inches long and her mate a finger-length smaller, but not nearly so small as the little blue darter, the sharp-shinned hawk, only about a foot in length, but which it very closely resembles in plumage and villainy. Both species have slaty-gray upper parts with deep bars across their wings and ashy-gray tails The latter differ in outline, however, Cooper's hawk having a rounded tail with whitish tip, and the sharp-shinned hawk a square tail. In maturity Cooper's hawk wears a blackish crown. Both species have white throats with dark streaks and the rest of their under parts are much barred with buff and white.

Instead of spending their time perching on lookouts, as the red-tailed and red-shouldered hawks do, these two reprobates dash after their victims on the wing, chasing them across open stretches where such swift, dexterous, dodging flyers are sure to overtake them. Or they will flash out of a clear sky like feathered lightning and boldly strike a chicken, though it be pecking corn near a farmer's feet. These two marauders, and the big slate-coloured goshawk, also called the blue hen hawk or partridge hawk, stab their cruel talons though the vitals of more valuable poultry, song and game birds, than any child would care to read about.

BALD EAGLE

Every American boy and girl knows our national bird, which is the farmer's ally, however, only when it appears on the money in his pocket. Without an eagle on that, you must know it would be of little use to him.

Truth to tell, this majestic emblem of our republic (borrowed from imperial Rome) that spreads itself gloriously over our coins, flag poles, public buildings and government documents, is, in real life, not the bravest of the brave, nor the most intelligent, nor the noblest, nor the most enterprising of birds, as one fain would believe. On the contrary, it often uses its wonderful eyesight to detect a bird more skilful than itself in the act of catching a fish, and then puts forth its superb strength to rob the successful fisher of his prey. The osprey is a frequent sufferer, although some of the water fowl, that patiently course over the waves hour after hour, in search of a dinner, may be robbed of it by the overpowering pirate. Dead fish cast up on the beach are not rejected. When fish fail, coots, ducks, geese and gulls—the fastest of flyers—are likely to be snatched up, plucked clean of their feathers, and torn apart by the great bird that drops suddenly upon them from the clouds like Jove's thunderbolt. Rarely small animals are seized, but there is probably no well-authenticated case of an eagle carrying off a child.

It is in their family life that hawks and eagles, however cruel at other times, show some truly lovable traits. Once mated, they know neither divorce nor family quarrels all their lives. Home is the dearest spot on earth to them. They become passionately attached to the great bundle of trash that is at once their nest and their abode. A tall pine tree, near water, or the rocky ledge of some steep cliff, is the favourite site for an eagle eyrie. Here the devoted mates will carry an immense quantity of sticks, sod, cornstalks, pine twigs, weeds, bones, and other coarse rubbish, until, after annual repairs for several seasons, the broad, flat nest may grow to be almost as high as it is wide and look something like a New York sky-scraper. Both parents sit on the eggs in turn and devote themselves with zeal to feeding the eaglets. These spoiled children remain in the nest several months without attempting to fly, expecting to be waited upon even after they are actually larger than the old birds. The castings of skins, bones, hair, scales, etc., in the vicinity of a hawk's or eagle's nest, will indicate, almost as well as Dr. Fisher's analysis, what food the babies had in their stomachs to make them grow so big. Immature birds are almost black all over. Not until they are three years old do the feathers on their heads and necks turn white, giving them the effect of being bald. Any eagle seen in the eastern United States is sure to be of this species.

In the West and throughout Asia and Africa lives the golden eagle, of which Tennyson wrote the lines that apply equally well to our Eastern "bird of freedom":

> "He clasps the crag with crooked hands;
> Close to the sun in lonely lands,
> Ringed with the azure world he stands.
> The wrinkled sea beneath him crawls:
> He watches from his mountain walls,
> And, like a thunderbolt, he falls."

AMERICAN SPARROW HAWK

Called also: Killy Hawk; Rusty-crowned Falcon;
Mouse Hawk

Just such an extended branch as a shrike or a kingbird would use as a lookout while searching the landscape o'er for something to eat, the little sparrow hawk chooses for the same purpose. He is not much larger than either of these birds, scarcely longer than a robin. Because he is a hawk, with the family possession of eyes that are both telescope and miscroscope, he can detect a mouse, sparrow, garter snake, spider or grasshopper, farther away than seems to us possible.

Every farmer's boy knows this beautiful little rusty-red hawk, with slaty-blue cap and wings, and creamy-buff spotted sides, if not by sight then by sound, as it calls *kill-ee, kill-ee kill-ee*, across the fields. It does not soar and revolve in a merry-go-round on high like its cousins, but flies swiftly and gracefully, keeping near enough to the ground to see everything that creeps or hops through the grass. Dropping suddenly, like a stone, upon its victim (usually a grasshopper) it seizes it in its small, sharp, fatal talons and bears it away to a favourite perch, there to enjoy it at leisure.

This is the hawk that is so glad to find a deserted woodpecker's hole for its nest. How many other birds gratefully accept those skilful carpenters' vacant tenements!

AMERICAN OSPREY

Called also: Fish Hawk

A pair of these beautiful big hawks, that had nested year after year in the top of a tall pine tree on the Manasquan River, New Jersey, were great pets in that region. An old fisherman of Barnegat Bay told me that when he was hauling in his seine one day, he saw the male osprey strike the water with a splash, struggle an instant with a great fish that had been following his net, and disappear below the waves, never to rise again. The bird more than met his match that time. The fish was far larger than he expected, so powerful that it easily dragged him under, once his talons were imbedded in the fish's flesh. For the rest of the summer the widowed osprey always stayed about when the fisherman hauled his net on the beach, and bore away to her nest the worthless fish he left in it for her special benefit. But after rearing her family—a prolonged process for all the hawks, eagles, and owls—she never returned to the neighbourhood. Perhaps old associations were too painful; perhaps she was shot on her way South that winter; or perhaps she took another mate with more sense and less greed, who preferred to reside elsewhere.

As you may imagine, fish hawks always live near water. In summer they frequent the inlets along the Atlantic coast, but over inland lakes and rivers also, many fly back and forth. You may know by their larger size—they are almost two feet long—and by their slow flight that they are not the winter gulls. Their dusky backs and white under parts harmonise well with the marine picture, North or South. Their plumage contains more white than that of any other hawk. No matter how foggy the day or how quietly the diving osprey may splash to catch his fish dinner, any bald-headed eagle in the vicinity is sure to detect him in the act of seizing it, and then to relieve him of it instantly.

OWLS

Like many children I know, owls begin to be especially lively toward night, only they make no noise as they fly about. Very soft, fluffy plumage muffles their flight so that they can drop upon a meadow mouse creeping through the grass in the stilly night before this wee, timorous beastie suspects there is a foe abroad. As owls live upon mice, mostly, it is important they should be helped to catch them with some device that beats our traps. If mice should change their nocturnal habits, the owl's whole scheme of existence would be upset, and the hawks would get the quarry that they now enjoy: mice, rats, moles, bats, frogs and the larger insects. You see the farmer has invaluable day and night allies in these birds of prey which take turns in protecting his fields from rodents, one patrol working while the other sleeps. On the whole, owls are the more valuable to him. They usually continue their good work all through the winter after the hawks have gone South. Can you think of any other birds that work for him at night?

Not only can owls fluff out their loose, mottled plumage, but they can draw it in so close as to change their shape and size in an instant, so that they look like quite different birds, or rather not like birds at all, but stumps of trees. Altering their outlines, changing their shape and size at will, is one of these queer birds' peculiarities. Their eyes, set in the centre of feathered discs, do not revolve in their sockets, but are so fixed that they look only straight ahead, which is why an owl must turn his head every time he wishes to glance to the right or left. Another peculiarity is the owls' method of eating. Bolting entire all the food they catch, head first, they digest only the nutritious portions of it. Then, bowing their heads and shaking them very hard, they eject the bones, claws, skin, hair and fur in matted pellets, without the least distress. Some children I know, who swallow their food in a hurry—cherry stones, grape skins, apple cores and all—need a similar, merciful digestive apparatus.

Like the hawks, owls are devoted, life-long mates. The females are larger than the males. Some like to live in dense evergreens that hide them from teasing blue jays and other foes by day; some, like the barn owl, prefer towers, church steeples or the tops of barns and other buildings; some hide in hollow trees or deserted woodpeckers' holes, but all naturally prefer to take their long, daily naps where the sunlight does not penetrate. They live in their homes more hours than woodpeckers or any other birds. No doubt we pass by many sleeping owls without suspecting their presence.

BARN OWL

Called also: Monkey-faced Owl

This is the shy, odd-looking, gray and white mottled owl with the triangular face and slim body, about a foot and a half long, that comes out of its hole at evening with a wild scream, startling timid and superstitious people into the belief that it is uncanny. The American counterpart of "wise Minerva's only fowl," its large eye-discs and solemn blink certainly make it look like a fit companion for the goddess of wisdom.

A tame barn owl, owned by a gentleman in Philadelphia, would sit on his shoulder for hours at a time. It felt offended if its master would not play with it. The only way the man could gain time for himself during the bird's waking hours, was to feed it well and leave a stuffed bird for it to play with when he went out of the room, just as Jimmy Brown left a doll with his baby sister when he went out to play; only the man could not tack the owl's petticoats to the floor.

A pair of barn owls lived for many years in the tower of the Smithsonian Institution, Washington. Dr. Fisher found the skulls of four hundred and fifty-four small mammals in the pellets cast about their home. Another pair lived in a tower and on the best of terms with some tame pigeons. Happily the owls had no taste for squab, but the debris of several thousand mice and rats about their curious dwelling proved that their appetite needed no coaxing with such a delicacy.

SHORT-EARED OWL

Called also: Marsh Owl; Meadow Owl

This owl, and its long-eared cousin, wear the tufts of feathers in their ears that resemble harmless horns. Unlike its relatives, the short-eared owl does some hunting by daylight, especially in cloudy weather, and like the marsh hawk it prefers to live in grassy, marshy places frequented by meadow mice. On the other hand, the long-eared owl respects family traditions, and goes about only after dark. "It usually spends the day in some evergreen woods, thick willow copse or alder swamp, although rarely it may be found in open places," says Dr. Fisher. "The bird is not wild and will allow itself to be closely approached. When conscious that its presence is recognised, it sits upright, draws the feathers close to its body, and erects the ear-tufts, resembling in appearance a piece of weather-beaten bark more than a bird." The long and the short of it is, that few people, except professional bird students, know very much about these or any other owls, for few find them by day or forsake their couches when they are abroad. We may take Dr. Johnson's advice and "give our days and nights to the study of Addison," but few of us give even a part of our days and less of our nights to the study of the birds about us.

BARRED OWL

Called also: Hoot Owl

If "a good child should be seen and not heard" what can be said for this owl? Its deep-toned *whoo-whoo-who-whoo-to-whoo-ah*, like the wail of some lost soul asking the way, is the only indication you are likely to have that a hoot owl lives in your neighbourhood. You can imitate its voice and deliberately "hoot it up." Few people who know its voice will ever see its smooth, round, bland, almost human face.

"As useless as a last year's nest" can have no meaning to a pair of these large hardy owls that go about toward the end of winter looking for a deserted woodpecker's nest or a hawk's, crow's, or squirrel's bulky cradle in some tree top. Ever after they hold it as their own.

Farmers shoot the owl that occasionally takes one of their broilers or a game bird, not knowing that the remainder of its diet really leaves them in its debt.

SCREECH OWLS

A boy I know had a pair of little screech owls invite themselves to live in a box he had nailed up for bluebirds in his father's orchard. Although they had full liberty, in time they became tame pets, even pampered darlings, with a willing slave to trap mice for them in the corn crib and hay loft. At first mice were plentiful enough, and every day after school the boy would empty the traps, climb the apple tree and feed the owls. But presently the mice learned the danger that may lurk behind an innocent looking lump of cheese. One foolish, hungry mouse now and then was all the boy could catch. This he would carry by the tail to his sleeping pets, arouse them by dangling it against their heads, at which, while half asleep, they would click their beaks like castanets. When both were wide awake he would allow one of them to bolt the mouse while he still held on firmly to the tail. Then, jerking the mouse back out of the owl's throat, he would allow the other owl to really swallow it. When next he caught a mouse, the operation was reversed: the owl that had been satisfied before now gulped the mouse first, only to have it jerked away and fed to its mate. In this way, strange to say, the boy kept on friendly terms with the pair for several weeks, when he discovered that they liked bits of raw beef quite as well as mice. After that he carried his queer pets to the house and kept them in his room all winter. Early in the spring they returned to the bird house and raised a family of funny, fluffy, plump little owlets.

This boy discovered for himself the screech owls' strange characteristic of changing their colour without changing their feathers, as moulting song birds change theirs. They have a rusty, reddish-brown phase and a mottled-gray phase. So far as is known, these changes of colour are not dependent upon age, sex, or season. No one understands what causes them or what they mean. Sometimes the same family will contain birds with plumage that is rusty-brown or gray or intermediate. But you may always know a screech owl by its small size (it is only about as long as a robin) and by the ear tufts that make it look wide-awake and very wise.

By day it keeps well hidden in some deserted woodpecker's hole or a hollow in some old orchard tree, which is its favourite residence; but some mischievous little birds, with sharper eyes than ours, often discover its hiding place, wake it up, and chase it, blinking and bewildered, all about the farm. By night, when its tormentors are asleep, this little owl goes forth for its supper, and then we hear its weird, sweet, shivering, tremulous cry. Because it lives near our homes and is, perhaps, the commonest of the owls all over our country, every child can know it by sound, if not by sight.

CHAPTER XVI

MOURNER, WHISTLER, AND DRUMMER

Mourning Dove
Bob-white
Ruffed Grouse

MOURNING DOVE

Called also: Carolina Dove

D⁰ NOT waste any sympathy on this incessant love-maker that slowly sings
coo-o-o, ah-coo-o-o-ooo-o-o-ooo-o-o, in a sweetly
sad voice. Really he is no more melancholy than the plaintive pewee but, on the
contrary, is so happy in his love that his devotion has passed into a proverb. Nevertheless, the song he sings to his "turtle dove"
sounds more like a dirge than a rapture. While
she lives, there is no more contented bird in the
woods.

Dove lovers are quite self-sufficient. Their
larger cousins, the wild pigeons, that once were
so abundant, depended on friends for much of
their happiness and lived in enormous flocks.
Now only a few pairs survive in this land of
liberty to refute the adage "In union there is
strength." Because millions of pigeons slept
in favourite roosts many miles in extent, they
were all too easily netted, and it did not take
greedy men long to turn the last flock into cash.
Happily, doves preserved their race by scat-
tering in couples over a wide area—from

Panama, in winter, as far north as Ontario in warm weather. Not until nursery duties, which begin early in the spring, are over, late in summer, do they give up their shy, unsocial habits to enjoy the company of a few friends. When they rise on whistling wings from tree-bordered fields, where they have been feeding on seeds and grain, not a gun is fired: no one cares to eat them.

Only the cuckoo of our common birds builds so flimsy a nest as the dove's adored darling. I am sorry to tell you she is a slack, incompetent housekeeper, but evidently her lover is blind to every fault. What must the expert phœbe think of such a poorly made, untidy cradle, or that bustling, energetic housewife, Jenny Wren, or the tiniest of clever architects, the humming-bird? It is a wonder that the dove's two white eggs do not fall through the rickety, rimless, unlined lattice. How scarred and bruised the naked bodies of the twins must be by the sticks! Like pigeons, hummingbirds, flickers, and some other feathered parents, doves feed their fledg-lings by pumping partly digested food—"pigeon's milk"—from their own crops into theirs.

When they leave the open woodlands to take a dust bath in the road, or to walk about and collect gravel for their interior grinding machines, or to get a drink of water before going to sleep, you may have a good look at them. As they walk, they bob their heads in a funny manner of their own. They are bluish, fawn-coloured birds about a foot long. The male has some exquisite metallic colours on his neck, otherwise he resembles his best beloved. Both wear black crescent patches on their cheeks. All the feathers on their long, pointed tails, except the two largest central ones, have a narrow, black band across the end and are tipped with white. The breast feathers shade from pinkish fawn to pale buff below. Beautiful birds these, in spite of their quiet, Quaker clothes.

BOB-WHITE

Called Also: "Quail-on-Toast"; Partridge

What a cheerful contrast is Bob White's clear, staccato whistle to the drawling coo of the amorous dove! Character is often expressed in a bird's voice as well as in ours. From their voices alone you might guess that the dove and the quail are no relation. They do not belong even to the same order, bobwhite being a scratching bird and having the ruffed grouse and barnyard chicken for his kin. Pheasants and turkeys are distantly related. In the South people call him a partridge; in

New England it is the ruffed grouse that is
known by that name; therefore, to save confusion, why not always give bob-white the
name by which he calls himself? The chickadee,
phœbe, peewee, towhee, whip-poor-will and
bobolink, who tell their names less plainly than
he, save every child who tries to know them
much trouble. Don't you wish every bird
would introduce himself?

The boy who

"Drives home the cows from the pasture,
   Up through the long, shady lane,
 Where the quail whistles loud in the wheat fields,
    That are yellow with ripening grain,"

probably "whistles up" those bob-whites on
his way home as you would start up the roosters
in the barnyard by imitating their crow. *Bob
White! Ah, Bob White!* rings from some plump
little feathered gallant on the outskirts of almost
any farm during the long nesting season.

A slight depression in some dry, grassy field
or a hole at the foot of an old stump or weed-
hedged wall will be lined with leaves and grasses
by both mates in May to receive from ten to
eighteen brilliant white eggs that are packed in,
pointed end downwards, to economise space.
If an egg were removed, it would be difficult
indeed to re-arrange the clutch with such
economy. Would it not be cruel to touch a

nest which the outraged owners would at once desert?

Just as baby chickens follow the mother about, so downy bob-whites run after both their parents and learn which seeds, grain, insects and berries they may safely eat. Man, with his gun and dog and mowing machines, is their worst enemy, of course; then comes the sly fox and sneaking weasel that spring upon them from ambush, and the hawk that drops upon them like a thunderbolt. Birds have enemies above, below, and on every side. Is it any wonder that they are timid and shy? A note of alarm from Mamma White summons the chicks, half-running, half-flying, to huddle close to her or to take shelter beneath her short wings. Their little grouse cousins find protection in a more original way. When the mother is busy sitting on a second or third clutch of eggs, it is Bob himself, a pattern of all the domestic virtues, who takes full charge of the family. When the last chicks are ready to join their older brothers and sisters, the bevy may contain three or four dozen birds, all devotedly attached to one another. At bed time they squat in a circle on the ground, tails toward the centre of the ring, heads pointing outward to detect an enemy coming from any direction. As if their vigilance were not enough, Bob usually remains outside the ring to act as sentinel. At the sign of danger the bunch of birds will rise with loud whirring of the wings, as suddenly as a bomb might burst.

From November onward, every gun in the country will be trained against them. There is sufficient reason for poor people, who rarely have any really good food, or enough to eat, shooting game birds in season; but who has any patience with the pampered epicures for whose order "quail-on-toast" are cooked by the hundred thousand at city clubs, restaurants, and private tables, already over-supplied? No *chef* could ever tempt me to eat this friendly little song bird that stays about the farm with his family through the coldest winter to pick up the buckwheat, cheap raisins, and sweepings from the hay loft that keep him as neighbourly as a robin. Every farmer who does not post his place, and who allows this useful ally in his eternal war against weeds and insect pests to be shot, impoverishes himself more than he is aware.

RUFFED GROUSE

Called also: Partridge

Bob-white and ruffed grouse are the fife and drum corps of the woods. That some birds are wonderful musicians everybody knows.

No other orchestra contains a member who can drum without a drum. Even that famous drummer, the woodpecker, needs a dead, dry, resonant, hardwood limb to tap on before he can produce his best effects. How does the grouse beat his deep, muffled, thump, thump, thumping, rolling tattoo? Some scientists have staked their reputation on the claim that they have seen him drum by rapidly striking his wings against the sides of his body; but other later-day scientists, who contend that he beats only the air when his wings vibrate so fast that the sight cannot quite follow them, are undoubtedly right.

On a fallen log, a stump, a rail fence or a wall, that may have been used as a drumming stand for many years, the male grouse will strut with a jerking, dandified gait, puff out his feathers, ruff his neck frills, raise and spread his fan-shaped tail like a turkey cock, blow out his cheeks and neck, then suddenly halt and begin to beat his wings. After a few slow, measured thumps, the stiff, strong wings whir faster and faster, until there is only a blur where they vibrate. This is the grouse's love song that summons a mate to their trysting place. It serves also as a challenge to a rival. Blood and feathers may soon be strewn around the ground, for in the spring grouse will fight as fiercely as game-cocks. Sportsmen in the autumn woods often hear grouse drumming at the old stand, merely from excess of vigour and not because they take the slightest interest then in a mate. After the mating season is over, they have less chivalry than barnyard roosters.

Shy, wary birds of wooded, hilly country, grouse are rarely thought of as possible pets, but the gentle little girl in the picture won the heart of a drummer and subdued his wildness, as you see. Some people are trying to domesticate grouse in wire-enclosed poultry yards.

Sometimes when, like "the cat that walked by himself" you wander "in the wild wet woods," perhaps you will be suddenly startled by the loud whirring roar of a big brown grouse that suddenly hurls itself from the ground near your feet. If it were shot from the mouth of a cannon it could surprise you no less. Then it sails away, dodging the trees and disappears. Gunners have "educated" the intelligent bird into being, perhaps, the most wily, difficult game in the woods.

Like the meadowlark, flicker, sparrows and other birds that spend much time on the ground, the bob-white and ruffed grouse wear brown feathers, streaked and barred, to harmonise perfectly with their surroundings. "To find a hen grouse with young is a memorable experience," says Frank M. Chapman. "While the parent is giving us a lesson in mother love and bird intelligence, her downy chicks are teaching us facts in protective colouration and heredity. How the old one limps and flutters! She can barely drag herself along the ground. But while we are watching her, what has become of the ten or a dozen little yellow balls we had almost stepped on? Not a feather do we see, until, poking about in the leaves, we find one little chap hiding here and another squatting there, all perfectly still, and so like the leaves in colour as to be nearly invisible."

CHAPTER XVII

BIRDS OF THE SHORE AND MARSHES

KILLDEER

IF YOU don't know the little killdeer plover, it is surely not his fault, for he is a noisy sentinel, always ready, night or day, to tell you his name. *Killdee, killdee,* he calls with his high voice when alarmed—and he is usually beset by fears, real or imaginary—but when at peace, his voice is sweet and low. Much persecution from gunners has made the naturally gentle birds of the shore and marshes rather shy and wild. Most plovers nest in the Arctic regions, where man and his wicked ways are unknown. When the young birds reach our land of liberty and receive a welcome of hot shot, the survivors learn their first lesson in shyness. Some killdeer, however, are hatched in the United States. No sportsman worthy the name would waste shot on a bird not larger than a robin; one, moreover, with musky flesh; yet I have seen scores of killdeer strung over the backs of gunners in tide-water Virginia. Their larger cousins, the black-breasted, the piping, the golden and Wilson's plovers, who travel from the tundras of the far North to South America and back again every year, have now become rare because too much cooked along their long route. You can usually tell a flock of plovers in flight by the crescent shape of the rapidly moving mass.

With a busy company of friends, the killdeer haunts broad tracts of grassy land, near water-uplands or lowlands, or marshy meadows beside the sea. Scattered over a chosen feeding ground, the plovers run about nimbly, nervously, looking for trouble as well as food. Because worms, which are their favourite supper, come out of the ground at nightfåll, the birds are especially active then. Grasshoppers, crickets, and other insects content them during the day.

SEMIPALMATED PLOVER

The killdeer, which is our commonest plover, has a little cousin scarcely larger than an English sparrow that is a miniature of himself, except that the semipalmated (half-webbed) or ring-necked plover has only one dark band across the upper part of his white breast, while the killdeer wears two black rings. This dainty little beach bird has brownish-gray upper parts so like the colour of wet sand, that, as he runs along over it, just in advance of the frothing ripples, he is in perfect harmony with his surroundings. Relying upon that fact for protection, he will squat behind a tuft of beach grass if you pass too near rather than risk flight.

When the tide is out, you may see the tiny forms of these common ring-necks mingled with the ever-friendly little sandpipers on the exposed sand bars and wide beaches where all keep up a constant hunt for bits of shell fish, fish eggs and sand worms.

General Greely found them nesting in Grinnell Land in July, the males doing most of the incubating as is customary in the plover family, whose females certainly have advanced ideas. Downy little chicks run about as soon after leaving the egg as they are dry. In August the advance guard of southbound flocks begin to arrive in the United States *en route* for Brazil—quite a journey in the world to test the fledgling's wings.

LEAST SANDPIPER

Across the narrow beach we flit,
    One little sandpiper and I;
And fast I gather, bit by bit,
    The scattered driftwood bleached and dry.
The wild waves reach their hands for it,
    The wild wind raves, the tide runs high,
As up and down the beach we flit,—
    `One little sandpiper and I.

Above our heads the sullen clouds
    Scud black and swift across the sky;
Like silent ghosts in misty shrouds
    Stand out the white light-houses high.
Almost as far as eye can reach
    I see the close-reefed vessels fly,
As fast we flit along the beach,—
    One little sandpiper and I.

I watch him as he skims along
    Uttering his sweet and mournful cry;
He starts not at my fitful song,
    Or flash of fluttering drapery.
He has no thought of any wrong;
    He scans me with a fearless eye.
Stanch friends are we, well-tried and strong,
    The little sandpiper and I.

Comrade, where wilt thou be to-night
    When the loosed storm breaks furiously?
My driftwood fire will burn so bright!
    To what warm shelter canst thou fly?
I do not fear for thee, though wroth
    The tempest rushes through the sky:
For are we not God's children both,
    Thou, little sandpiper, and I?

Almost every child I know is more familiar
with Celia Thaxter's poem about the little sandpiper than with the bird itself. But if you have
the good fortune to be at the seashore in the
late summer, when flocks of the friendly mites
come to visit us from the Arctic regions on their
way south, you can scarcely fail to become
acquainted with the companion of Mrs. Thaxter's lonely walks along the beach at the Isles
of Shoals where her father kept the lighthouse.

The least sandpipers, peeps, ox-eyes or stints, as they are variously called, are only about the size of sparrows—too small for any self-respecting gunner to bag, therefore they are still abundant. Their light, dingy-brown and gray, finely speckled backs are about the colour of the mottled sand they run over so nimbly, and their breasts are as white as the froth of the waves that almost never touch them. Beach birds become marvellously quick in reckoning the fraction of a second when they must run from under the combing wave about to break over their little heads. Plovers rely on their fleet feet to escape a wetting. Least sandpipers usually fly upward and onward if a deluge threatens; but they have a cousin, the semipalmated (half-webbed) sandpiper that swims well when the unexpected water suddenly lifts it off its feet.

These busy, cheerful, sprightly little peepers are always ready to welcome to their flocks other birds—ring-necked plovers, turnstones, snipe and phalaropes. If by no other sign, you may distinguish sandpipers by their constant call, *peep-peep*.

SPOTTED SANDPIPER

Do you know the spotted sandpiper, teeter, tilt-up, teeter-tail, teeter-snipe, or tip-up, whichever you may choose to call it? As if it had not yet decided whether to be a beach bird or a woodland dweller, a wader or a perching songster, it is equally at home along the seashore or on wooded uplands, wherever ditches, pools, streams, creeks, swamps, and wet meadows furnish its favourite foods. It stays with us through the long summer. Did you ever see it go through any of the queer motions that have earned for it so many names? Jerking up first its head, then its tail, it walks with a funny, bobbing, tipping, see-saw gait, as if it were self-conscious and conceited. Still another popular name was given from its sharp call *peet-weet*, *peet-weet*, rapidly repeated, and usually uttered as the bird flies in graceful curves over the water or inland fields.

WOODCOCK

Called also: Blind, Wall-eyed, Mud, Bigheaded, Wood, and Whistling Snipe; Bog-sucker; Bogbird; Timber Doodle

Whenever you see little groups of clean-cut holes dotted over the earth in low, wet ground, you may know that either the woodcock or Wilson's snipe has been there probing for worms. Not even the woodpecker's combination tool is more wonderfully adapted to its work than the bill of these snipe, which is a long, straight boring instrument, its upper half fitted with a flexible tip for hooking the worm out of its hole as you would lift a string out of a jar on your hooked finger. Down goes the bill into the mud, sunk to the nostrils; then the upper tip feels around for its slippery victim. You need scarcely hope to see the probing performance because earth-worms, like mice, come out of their holes after dark, which is why snipe are most active then.

A little boy once asked me this conundrum of his own making: "What is the difference between Martin Luther and a woodcock?" Just a few differences suggested themselves, but I did not guess right the very first time; can you? "One didn't like a Diet of Worms and the other does," was the small boy's answer.

After the ground freezes hard in the northern United States and Canada, the woodcock is compelled to go south of Virginia. But by the time the skunk cabbage and bright-green, fluted leaves of hellebore are pushing through the bogs and wet woodlands in earliest spring, back he comes again. An odd-looking, thick-necked, chunky fellow he is, less than a foot in length, his long, straight, stout bill sticking far out from his triangular head; his eyes placed so far back in the upper corners that he must be able to see behind him quite as well as he can look ahead; the streaks and bars of his mottled russet-brown, gray and buff and black upper parts being so laid on that he is in perfect harmony with the russet leaves, earth and underbrush of his woodland home. When his mate is sitting on her nest, the mimicry of her surroundings is so perfect it is well-nigh impossible to find her.

Sportsmen pursue both the woodcock and Wilson's snipe relentlessly, but happily they are no easy targets. Rising on short, stiff, whistling wings they fly in a zig-zag, erratic flight, and quickly drop to cover again, continually breaking the scent for a pursuing dog.

RAILS

Rails are such shy, skulking hiders among the tall marsh grasses that "every child" need never hope to know them all; but a few members of the family that are both abundant and noisy, may be readily recognised by their voices alone.

All rails prefer to escape from an intruder through the sedges in well-worn runways rather than trust their short, rounded wings to bear them beyond danger; and for forcing their way through grassy jungles, their narrow-breasted, wedge-shaped bodies are perfectly adapted. Compressed almost to a point in front, but broad and blunt behind where their queer little short-pointed tails stand up, the rails' small figures thread their way in and out of the mazes over the oozy ground with wonderful rapidity.

"As thin as a rail" means much to the cook who plucks one. It offers even a smaller bite than a robin to the epicure. When a gunner routs a rail it reluctantly rises a few feet above the grasses, flies with much fluttering, trailing its legs after it, but quickly sinks in the sedges again. Except in game bags, you rarely see a rail's varied brown and gray back or its barred breast. The bill is longer than the head. The long, widespread, flat toes help the owner to tread a dinner out of the mud as well as to swim across an inlet; and the short hind toes enable him to cling when he runs up the rushes to reach the tassels of grain at the top. No doubt you once played with some mechanical toy that made a noise something like the peculiar, rolling cackle of the clapper rail. This "marsh hen," which is common in the salt meadows along our coast from Long Island southward, continually betrays itself by its voice; otherwise you might never suspect its presence unless you are in the habit of pushing a punt up a creek to get acquainted with the

interesting shy creatures that dwell in what
Thoreau called "Nature's sanctuary."

The clapper's cousin, the sora, or Carolina
rail, so well known to gunners, alas! if not to
"every child," delights to live wherever wild
rice grows along inland lakes and rivers or
along the coast. Its sweetly whistled spring
song *ker-wee, ker-wee,* and "rolling whinny"
give place in autumn to the *'kuk, kuk, 'k-'k-'k-
'kuk* imitated by alleged sportsmen in search
of a mere trifle of flesh that they fill with shot.
As Mrs. Wright says of the bobolinks (neighbours of the soras in the rice fields) so may it
be written of them; they only serve "to length-
en some weary dinner where a collection of
animal and vegetable bric-a-brac takes the
place of satisfactory nourishment."

GREAT BLUE HERON

Standing motionless as the sphinx, with his
neck drawn in until his crested head rests
between his angular shoulders, the big, long-
legged, bluish-gray heron depends upon his
stillness and protective colouring to escape the
notice of his prey, and of his human foes (for
he has no others). In spite of his size—and he
stands four feet high without stockings—it takes
the sharpest eyes to detect him as he waits in

some shallow pool among the sedges along the creek or river side, silently, solemnly, hour after hour, for a little fish, frog, lizard, snake, or some large insect to come within striking distance. With a sudden stroke of his long, strong, sharp bill, he either snaps up his victim, or runs it through. A fish will be tossed in the air before being swallowed, head downward, that the fins may not scratch his very long, slender throat. When you are eating ice cream, don't you wish your throat were as long as this heron's?

A gunner, who wantonly shoots at any living target, will usually try to excuse himself for striking down this stately, picturesque bird into a useless mass of flesh and feathers, by saying that herons help themselves to too many fish. (He forgets about all the mice and reptiles they destroy.) But perhaps birds, as well as men, are entitled to a fair share of the good things of the Creator. Some people would prefer the sight of this majestic bird to the small, worthless fish he eats. What do you think about protecting him by law? Any one may shoot him now. The broad side of a barn would be about as good a test of a marksman's skill.

The evil that birds do surely lives after them; the good they do for us is far too little appreciated. Almost the last snowy heron and the last egret of Southern swamps have yielded their bodies to the knife of the plume hunter, who cuts out the exquisite decorations these birds wear during the nesting season. Inasmuch as all the heron babies depend upon their parents through an unusually long, helpless infancy, the little orphans are left to die by starvation. For what end is the slaughter of the innocents? Merely that the unthinking heads of vain women may be decked out with aigrettes! Don't blame the poor hunters too much when the plumes are worth their weight in gold.

LITTLE GREEN HERON

Called also: Poke; Chuckle-head

This most abundant member of his tropical tribe that spends the summer with us, is a shy, solitary bird of the swamps where you would lose your rubber boots in the quagmire if you attempted to know him too intimately. But you may catch a glimpse of him as he wades about the edge of a pond or creek with slow, calculated steps, looking for his supper. All herons become more active toward evening because their prey does. By day, this heron, like his big, blue cousin, might be mistaken for a stump or snag among the sedges and bushes by the waterside, so dark and still is he. Herons are accused of the tropical vice of laziness; but surely a bird that travels from northern Canada to the tropics and back again every year to earn its living, as the little green heron does, is not altogether lazy. Startle him, and he springs into the air with a loud *squawk*, flapping his broad wings and trailing his greenish-yellow legs behind him, like the storks you see painted on Japanese fans.

He and his mate have long, dark-green crests on their odd-shaped, receding heads and some lengthened, pointed feathers between the shoulders of their green or grayish-green hunched backs. Their figures are rather queer. The reddish-chestnut colour on their necks fades into the brownish-ash of their under parts, divided by a line of dark spots on the white throat that widen on the breast. Although the little green heron is the smallest member of this tribe of large birds that we see in the Northern States and Canada, it is about a foot and a half long, larger than any bird, except one of its own cousins, that you are likely to see in its marshy haunts.

Unlike many of their kind a pair of these herons prefer to build their rickety nests apart by themselves rather in one of those large, sociable, noisy and noisome colonies which we associate with the heron tribe. Flocking is sometimes a fatal habit.

BLACK-CROWNED NIGHT HERON

Called also: Quawk; Qua Bird

When the night herons return to us from the South in April, they go straight to the home of their ancestors, to which they are devotedly attached—rickety, ramshackle heronries, mere bundles of sticks in the tops of trees in some swamp—and begin at once to repair them. The cuckoo's and the dove's nests are fine pieces of architecture compared with a heron's. Is it not a wonder that the helpless heron babies do not tumble through the loose twigs? When they are old enough to climb around their latticed nursery, they still make no attempt to leave it, and several more weeks must pass before they attempt to fly. If there is an ancient heronry in your neighbourhood, as there is in mine, don't attempt to visit the untidy, ill-smelling place on a hot day. One would like to spray the entire colony with a deodoriser.

Thanks to the night heron's habits that keep him concealed by day when gunners are abroad, a few large heronries still exist within an hour's ride of New York, in spite of much persecution.

Unlike the solitary little green cousin, the black-crowned heron delights in company, and a hundred noisy pairs may choose to nest in some favourite spot. How they squawk over their petty quarrels! Wilson likened the noise to that of "two or three hundred Indians choking one another."

Only when they have young fledglings to feed do these herons hunt for food in broad daylight. But as the light fades they become increasingly active and noisy; even after it is pitch dark, when the fishermen go eeling, you may hear them *quawking* continually as they fly up and down the creek. Big, pearly-gray birds (they stand fully two feet high) with black-crowned heads, from which their long, narrow, white wedding feathers fall over the black top of the back, the night herons so harmonise with the twilight as to seem a part of it.

AMERICAN BITTERN

Called also: Stake-driver; Poke; Freckled Heron; Booming Bittern; Indian Hen

Even if you have never seen this shy hermit of large swamps and marshy meadows you must know him by his remarkable "barbaric yawp." Not a muscle does this brown and blackish and

buff freckled fellow move as he stands waiting
for prey to come within striking distance of
what appears to be a dead stump.   Sometimes
he stands with his head drawn in until it rests
on his back; or, he may hold his head erect and
pointed upward when he looks like a sharp
snag.   While he meditates pleasantly on the
flavour of a coming dinner, he suddenly snaps
and gulps, filling his lungs with air, then loudly
bellows forth the most unmusical bird cry you
are ever likely to hear.   You may recognise it
across the marsh half a mile away or more.   A
nauseated child would go through no more con-
vulsive gestures than this happy hermit makes
every time he lifts up his voice to call, *pump-
er-lunk*,   *pump-er-lunk*,   *pump-er-lunk*.   Still
another noise has earned him one of his many
popular names because it sounds like a stake
being driven into the mud.

A booming bittern I know sits hour after
hour, almost every day in summer, year after
year, on a dark, decaying pile of an old dock
in the creek.   Our canoe glides over the water
so silently it rarely disturbs him.   The timid
bird relies on his protective colouring to conceal him in so exposed a place and profits by
his fearlessness in broad daylight next to an
excellent feeding ground.   At low tide he walks
about sedately on the muddy flats treading out
a dinner.   Kingfishers rattle up and down the

creek, cackling rails hide in the sedges behind it, red-winged blackbirds flute above the phalanxes of rushes on its banks: but the bittern makes more noise, especially toward evening, than all the other inhabitants of the swampy meadows except the frogs, whose voices he forever silences when he can. Frogs, legs and all, are his favourite delicacy.

CHAPTER XVIII

THE FASTEST FLYERS

CANADA GOOSE

O F THE millions of migrants that stream across the sky every spring and autumn, none attract so much attention as the wild geese. How their mellow *honk, honk* thrills one when the birds pass like ships in the night! Such big, strong, rapid flyers have little to fear in travelling by daylight too, but gunners have taught them the wisdom of keeping up so high that they look like mere specks. It must be a very dull child without imagination, who is not stirred by the flight of birds that are launched on a journey of at least two thousand miles. Don't you wish you were as familiar with the map as these migrants must be? Usually geese travel in a wedge-shaped flock, headed by some old, experienced leader; but sometimes, with their long necks outstretched, they follow one another in Indian file and shoot across the clouds as straight as an arrow.

Geese spend much more time on land than ducks do. If you will study the habits of the common barnyard goose you will learn many of the ways of its wild relations that nest too far north to be watched by "every child." Canada geese that have been wounded by sportsmen in the fall, can be kept on a farm perfectly contented all winter; but when the honking flocks return from the south in March or April, they rarely resist " the call of the wild," and away they go toward their kin and freedom.

WILD DUCKS

Birds that spend their summers for the most part north of the United States and travel past us faster than the fastest automobile racer or locomotive—and an hundred miles an hour is not an uncommon speed for ducks to fly—need have little to fear, you might suppose.   But so mercilessly are they hunted whenever they stop to rest, that few birds are more timid.

River and pond ducks, that have the most delicious flavour because they feed on wild rice, celery and other dainty fare, frequent sluggish streams and shallow ponds.   There they tip up their bodies in a funny way to probe about the muddy bottoms, their heads stuck down under water, their tails and flat, webbed feet in the air directly above them, just as you have seen barnyard ducks stand on their heads. They like to dabble along the shores, too, and draw out roots, worms, seeds and tiny shellfish imbedded in the banks.   Of course they get a good deal of mud in their mouths, but fortunately their broad, flat bills have strainers on the sides, and merely by shutting them tight, the mud and water are forced out of the gutters. After nightfall they seem especially active and noisy.

In every slough where mallards, blue- and green-winged teal, widgeons, black duck and pintails settle down to rest in autumn, gunners wait concealed in the sedges. Decoying the sociable birds by means of painted wooden images of ducks floating on the water near the blind, they commence the slaughter at daybreak. But ducks are of all targets the most difficult, perhaps, for the tyro to hit. On the slightest alarm they bound from the water on whistling wings and are off at a speed that only the most expert shot overtakes. No self-respecting sportsman would touch the little wood duck—the most beautiful member of its family group. It is as choicely coloured and marked as the Chinese mandarin duck, and a possible possession for every one who has a country place with woods and water on it. Unlike its relatives, the wood duck nests in hollow trees and carries its babies to the water in its mouth as a cat carries its kittens.

The large group of sea and bay ducks, contains the canvas-back, red-head and other vegetarian ducks, dear to the sportsman and epicure. These birds may, perhaps, be familiar to "every child" as they hang by the necks in butcher-shop windows, but rarely in life. Enormous flocks once descended upon the Chesapeake Bay region. To Virginia and Maryland, therefore, hastened all the gunners in the East until the canvas-back, at least, is even more rare in the sportsman's paradise than it is on the gourmand's plate. Every kind of duck is now served up as canvas-back. Some sea ducks, however, which are fish eaters, have flesh too tough, rank, and oily for the table. They dive for their food, often to a great depth, pursuing and catching fish under water like the saw-billed mergansers or shelldrakes which form a distinct group. The surf scoters, or black coots, so abundant off the Atlantic coast in winter, dive constantly to feed on mussels, clams or scallops. Naturally such athletic birds are very tough.

With the exception of the wood duck, all ducks nest on the ground. Twigs, leaves and grasses form the rude cradle for the eggs, and, as a final touch of devotion, the mother bird plucks feathers from her own soft breast for the eggs to lie in. When there is any work to be done the selfish, dandified drakes go off by themselves, leaving the entire care of raising the family to their mates. Then they moult and sometimes lose so many feathers they are unable to fly. But by the time the ducklings are well grown and strong of wing, the drake joins the family, one flock joins another, and the ducks begin their long journey southward. But very few children, even in Canada, can ever hope to know them in their inaccessible swampy homes.

HERRING GULL

Called also: Winter Gull

"Every child" who has crossed the ocean or even a New York ferry in winter, knows the big, pearly-gray and white gulls that come from northern nesting grounds in November, just before the ice locks their larder, to spend the winter about our open waterways. On the great lakes and the larger rivers and harbours along our coast, you may see the scattered flocks sailing about serenely on broad, strong wings, gliding and skimming and darting with a poetry of motion few birds can equal. There are at least three things one never tires of watching: the blaze of a wood fire, the breaking of waves on a beach, and the flight of a flock of gulls.

Not many years ago gulls became alarmingly scarce. Why? Because silly girls and women, to follow fashion, trimmed their hats with gull's wings until hundreds of thousands of these birds and their exquisite little cousins, the terns or sea-swallows, had been slaughtered. Then some people said the massacre must stop and happily the law now says so too. Paid keepers patrol some of the islands where gulls and terns nest, which is the reason why you may see ashy-brown young gulls in almost every flock. When they mature, a deep-pearl mantle covers their backs and wings, and their breasts, heads and tails become snowy white. Their colouring now suggests fogs and white-capped waves.

Why protect birds that are not fit for food and that kill no mice nor insects in the farmer's fields? is often asked. A wise man once said "the beautiful is as useful as the useful," but the picturesque gulls are not preserved merely to enliven marine pictures and to please the eye of travellers. They fill the valuable office of scavengers of the sea. Lobsters and crabs, among many other creatures under the ocean, gulls, terns and petrels, among many creatures over it, do for the water what the turkey buzzard does for the land—rid it of enormous quantities of refuse. When one watches hundreds of gulls following the garbage scows out of New York harbour, or sailing in the wake of an ocean liner a thousand miles or more away from land, to pick up the refuse thrown overboard from the ship's kitchen, one realises the excellence of Dame Nature's housecleaning.

Gulls are greedy creatures. No sooner will one member of a flock swoop down upon a morsel of food, than a horde of hungry companions, in hot pursuit, chase after him to try to frighten him into dropping his dinner. With a harsh, laughing cry, *akak, kak, akak, kak, kak,* they wheel and float about a feeding ground for hours at a time.

And they fly incredibly far and fast. A flock that has followed an ocean greyhound all day will settle down to sleep at night "bedded" on the rolling water like ducks while "rocked in the cradle of the deep." After a rest that may last till dawn, they rise refreshed, fly in the direction of the vanished steamer and actually overtake it with apparent ease in time to pick up the scraps from the breakfast table. Reliable sailors say the same birds follow a ship from our shores all the way across the Atlantic.

INDEX

INDEX